Main Street

Welcome to Camden Falls

Also by Ann M. Martin

Belle Teal

A Corner of the Universe

A Dog's Life

Here Today

On Christmas Eve

P.S. Longer Letter Later
written with Paula Danziger

Snail Mail No More
written with Paula Danziger

Ten Kids, No Pets

The Baby-sitters Club series

Main Street

Welcome to Camden Falls

Ann M. Martin

SCHOLASTIC INC.

NEW YORK ◇ TORONTO ◇ LONDON ◇ AUCKLAND ◇ SYDNEY
MEXICO CITY ◇ NEW DELHI ◇ HONG KONG ◇ BUENOS AIRES

This book is for Valerie Portolano

ISBN-13: 978-0-545-14305-9
ISBN-10: 0-545-14305-5

12 11 10 9 8 7 6 5 4 3 2 1   8 9 10 11 12 13/0

Printed in the U.S.A.   40

First Book Club paperback printing, November 2008

Illustrations by Dan Andreason

The author would like to thank Samuel Nagler for his suggestions and his sensitive evaluation of the manuscript.

CHAPTER I

Main Street

Flora, curled in the backseat of Min's car, thought of all the orphaned children she'd read about in books — boys and girls without any parents, starting new lives in new places — and now she, Flora Marie Northrop, was one of them. Outside the window of Min's Toyota, the scenery flew by, a blur of branches and green leaves, bits of clouds, patches of clear New England sky. Flora turned and poked her sister, hoping for a game, a joke, anything to relieve the monotony of this seemingly endless trip. But Ruby remained stubbornly asleep, one hand resting on a carrier that held their cat, King Comma, who was also asleep.

Flora sighed, sat up, and peered into the front seat. Her grandmother drove steadily, humming along to "An American in Paris," the first selection on her *Gershwin Favorites* CD. Next to her dozed Daisy Dear, her plume of a tail sweeping back and forth across the seat as she dreamed a doggy dream.

Flora resumed her position between King and the window. She was nothing, she thought, like the orphans she had read about. For starters, most of them were British. And when they began their new lives, horrible things happened to them: They were sent to freezing, nasty orphanages where they lived in long rooms lined with flea-infested beds and were served only water and gruel for each meal. Either that or they had to go on grand quests for truth or power or lost family treasures, trekking through mist and mountains and muck, facing dragons and giants.

Flora and Ruby were not pale waifs shivering under threadbare blankets. Nor were they off on a glorious, romantic adventure. They were just Flora and Ruby Northrop, whose parents had died in a car accident and who were now going to live with their grandmother Min in Camden Falls, Massachusetts.

In the five months since the accident, Flora had discovered something that was fascinating and horrible at the same time: If she willed herself *not* to think about the accident, then she truly could put it out of her mind. This was harder than it sounded. It was like telling yourself not to poke a loose tooth with your tongue. But Flora could do it; she could put the accident right out of her mind if she gave herself the order. On the other hand — and this was what was most horrible and fascinating — when she wanted to remember the accident, as she did on certain days, then she could transport herself back to that awful, unforgettable night and recall it detail for detail.

It had been early on a frosty January evening, a Friday. Not quite dinnertime yet, but already night had fallen.

"Everyone hop in the car," her father had said. "We'll go out for pizza."

Flora hadn't wanted to go. Instead, she'd wanted to finish all of her homework then, right then, so she could have the entire weekend free.

"Oh, come on, Florrie Dorrie," her father had said, which had made Flora cross because Florrie Dorrie was such a babyish nickname, and she was about to turn eleven. She *had* hopped into the car, but she was grumbling, which was unusual for her, and her bad mood did not improve when she heard her mother say quietly to her father, a smile in her voice, that Flora must be turning into a teenager already.

They drove slowly down their street, past the familiar houses, a soft snow falling that you could really only see in the headlights or streetlights. When they drove by Annika's house, Flora had tried to look in the living room window, hoping for a glimpse of her best friend.

Then they had turned onto Maverick Way, a busier road than their own, and Flora's mother had said, "Come on, let's sing. Last chance for Christmas carols."

Ruby, who was eight then, had thought this was a wonderful idea. Of course she had. Ruby loved to sing, loved to dance, loved to be onstage. "'Winter Wonderland'!" she had cried, but before she could get the first word out, before anybody could say or do anything more, a truck traveling toward them, traveling too fast for a snowy evening, crossed over the centerline and thundered into their car. The next few moments were bright lights and crunching glass and tearing metal, but no screams — only Ruby's startled "Oh!"

The rescue workers arrived quickly. They pulled Flora and Ruby from the backseat, dazed but unhurt, still buckled into their seat belts. The girls were taken to the hospital in an ambulance, just to be on the safe side. Their parents were taken in a second ambulance.

It wasn't until later that evening that a police officer led Flora and Ruby to a small room in the hospital, handed each of them a teddy bear, and asked Flora if she knew the name of a person to call in an emergency. "Annika's mother," Flora had said, and discovered that her teeth were chattering even though she wasn't cold. "Mrs. Lindgren." When the officer asked about a relative, Flora had said, "Min. I mean, Mindy Read. That's our grandmother." And she had even been able to recall Min's phone number, including the area code.

At this point, Flora's precise memories became hazy. Who had collected her and Ruby from the hospital?

And who had told them that their parents had died? Min? When had she arrived? Very late that night, Flora thought, but she wasn't sure. All she truly remembered about the rest of the evening was that after she had learned her parents were gone, her mind turned numb the way her foot sometimes did in the middle of the night, and so a lot of things after that were unclear to her, even now.

There had been a funeral, of course, and Flora and Ruby had stayed out of school for a while, but eventually Min said they must try to get their lives back in order, which seemed impossible. There they were, Flora and Ruby, living in their own house, but with their grandmother and her golden retriever instead of with their parents. And nothing was the same, no matter how Min tried to make it so.

From the very start, Min, who was the girls' legal guardian — it said so in the Northrops' will — had told Flora and Ruby that she was going to stay with them in their house while they finished out the school year. "You'll be right here on your old street with your old friends," she had said. But she had also said that when summer came, they would be moving to Camden Falls. The town was Min's home, after all. Her house, which had been in her family since long before she was born, was plenty big enough to accommodate Flora and Ruby and King Comma. It was the house in which

Min and her husband had raised the girls' mother and her younger sister. Needle and Thread, the sewing store on Main Street that Min owned and ran with her friend Mrs. Walter, was in Camden Falls, too. In other words, Min's life was there. And as much as she loved her granddaughters, she couldn't see leaving her home and moving to a strange town where she had, among other things, no friends and no work. Better to bring Ruby and Flora back to Camden Falls with her.

Flora had protested this decision quietly. Ruby had protested it loudly.

"*You* don't want to leave *your* friends and *your* home, but you're making *us* leave *our* friends and *our* home," Ruby had exclaimed more than once in her most dramatic voice. "And *you're* the *grown*-up."

Min was patient. "I understand, Ruby," she had said. "And I know you're sad. I'm sad, too. We've all lost people we care about. I never dreamed I'd outlive my daughter. But we do have to move on. We have to make a life for ourselves, and I need to support you and Flora. That's why I have to go back to Needle and Thread."

Min was nothing if not practical. And busy. She was always busy. Which was why Flora, when she was very small, had started calling her not Gran or Granny or Grandma, but Min. Min wasn't short for Mindy — it was short for "In a minute."

"Come see my new hat," Flora would say when Min was visiting.

"In a minute," her grandmother would reply.

"Can you read to me?"

"In a minute."

Flora's name for her had stuck, and soon everyone called her Min. Now busy, practical Min was trying to settle down with her granddaughters. Since January, she had lived in their home with them and King Comma. She had mended their school clothes and gone to parent-teacher conferences and fixed meals and helped with homework. As often as she could, though, she had piled the girls and King Comma and Daisy Dear into the car and made the long trip back to Camden Falls. They would spend the weekend there while Min checked on her house and the store, and the girls selected the rooms that would be their bedrooms and talked to Mrs. Walter's granddaughter Olivia, who lived next door.

Time had passed, and suddenly it was June. Amazing, Flora thought. A little over five months had gone by since the night of the accident. School had ended, Min had sold their house and most of their things, Flora and Ruby had said good-bye to Annika and the rest of their friends, and now they were making a final, one-way trip to Camden Falls.

So here was Flora, curled in the backseat with the sleeping Ruby and King Comma, while in the front, Min drove purposefully on, Daisy Dear at her side. A U-Haul lurched along behind the car, loaded with the girls' clothes and bedroom furniture, their toys and books and games, Ruby's tap shoes, and Flora's art supplies.

Flora and Ruby, orphans, were on the way to their new lives.

"Ah! Here we go!" Min called gaily from the front seat. "The Mass Pike. We're almost there."

Ruby stirred and opened her eyes. "The turnpike?" she mumbled. "How many more hours?"

"Just a couple," Min replied.

"I'm bored," said Ruby.

"You've been asleep," Flora pointed out. "How can you be bored?"

"I just am."

"Let's sing songs," said Min, and she pushed the button to turn off her CD. "How about a round? How about 'Tender Shepherd'? I'll start."

Ruby and Flora joined in listlessly.

Finally, Ruby announced that she was bored again.

"Want to play the license plate game?" Flora asked.

Ruby shook her head.

"Anyone need a bathroom break?" asked Min. "Wait. I have an idea."

"What?" asked Ruby.

"You'll see."

A few minutes later, Min pulled off the turnpike. "I think we need ice cream," she said. She drove around a small town until she came to a weathered wooden building sitting alone at the end of a narrow lane. A sign by the door read:

THE SNACK SHACK
Food
Ice Cream
Souvenirs
Gas
Worms (bait)

"Well, this looks like the place for us," said Min.

"I guess I *could* use some worms," said Flora, which made Ruby and Min laugh.

Min parked the car and everyone rolled down the windows so King and Daisy would have plenty of air. Flora and Ruby climbed stiffly out of the car and stretched their legs, while Min said, "You be good, Daisy Dear. No barking while we're gone."

Ruby opened the door to the Snack Shack. Inside was one big room crowded with shelves of souvenirs. Along the back wall was a counter with eight red stools lined in front of it. Behind the counter stood a man with silver hair wearing a greasy apron that might have been white or gray or brown. It was hard to tell.

"Greetings, folks!" said the man. "I'm Phil. Welcome to the Snack Shack. What can I get for you?"

"Ice-cream sundaes," said Min firmly, "all around."

"Ice-cream *sun*daes?" repeated Ruby.

"Really?" said Flora.

"It's a special occasion," replied Min.

Phil made three sundaes and said that Min and the girls were welcome to eat them outside at the picnic table.

So they did. Flora kept an eye on the car. She suspected that King was hissing in his carrier. Ruby looked at the sky, at the pine trees, and breathed in deeply. "It smells different here than at home," she said.

"This is New England," said Min proudly.

Back in the Snack Shack, after Min and Ruby and Flora had scraped every last bit of ice cream from their dishes and returned them to Phil, Min said, "Why don't you each choose a souvenir? Something to remember this trip by."

Flora could feel her lower lip tremble. She wasn't sure she wanted something to remember this trip by. But she didn't want to hurt Min's feelings. She turned away, wandered up and down the aisles, fingered pine pillows and tallow candles, and looked at a display of maple syrup jugs. Ruby eyed the penny candy.

In the end, Flora chose a small box containing a single piece of maple sugar candy and Ruby chose a bag of Mary Janes and jawbreakers. The souvenirs would be gone by the next day. Flora saw that Min knew this, but nobody said anything. They thanked Phil and returned to the car.

Min drove on. Flora and Ruby sat silently, gazing out the windows. After a while, Ruby sighed hugely and said, "How much *long*er is this *trip* going to *take*?"

"No whining," said Min. "And the answer to your question is about fifteen minutes. Look. There's our exit."

Min steered the car off the turnpike. The U-Haul rumbling behind, they drove along a smaller highway, then along Route 6A, with the ponds and beaver dams on one side, the thick maple trees on the other.

At last, Ruby said softly, "There it is."

Flora saw the sign that read WELCOME TO CAMDEN FALLS. She felt her lip start to tremble again, felt her stomach drop. This was it. This was the very end of her old life — and the very beginning of her new life.

She willed herself not to cry. And then she felt Ruby's hand in hers and gripped it.

Min glanced in the rearview mirror at her granddaughters. "Ready?" she asked.

She pulled up to an intersection. A green sign ahead of them read LAWRENCE with an arrow pointing to the left, and CAMDEN FALLS with an arrow pointing to the right. Min turned right, then right again, and Main Street stretched ahead.

CHAPTER 2

Mary Woolsey

Old Mary Woolsey sat on a bench in front of Needle and Thread. It was a fine, warm Saturday in June, and she had no customers in the store at the moment. Sometimes when things were slow, she liked to sit outside, even in cold weather. Evelyn Walter and Min Read, the owners of the store, didn't mind. Often, one of them would bring her coffee or tea while she sat.

Mary knew that lots of people in Camden Falls, especially the children, thought she was strange. They rarely spoke to her unless something needed mending or altering. That was all right with Mary. She liked to sit quietly and watch. She had learned an awful lot about Camden Falls and its people just by watching.

For instance, over there was Lydia Malone, who lived next door to Min Read in the Row Houses. Lydia was a teenager now, thirteen or fourteen maybe, and

Mary had a strong suspicion that she was going to get into some kind of trouble this summer. It was those kids she'd been hanging around with. And over there was sad Nikki Sherman, who lived way out in the country with that bad-news family of hers. Who had brought Nikki into town today? She seemed to be alone. Crossing the street now was kind Mr. Pennington, who also lived in one of the Row Houses. He tipped his hat to Mary as he walked by. And here came Sonny Sutphin, steering himself awkwardly along the sidewalk, one gloved hand pushing the right wheel on his chair, his left foot dragging on the pavement for reasons Mary didn't understand, since there was nothing wrong with the footrest on the wheelchair.

Mary's gaze shifted to the right. She watched as a car turned onto Main Street. The car was towing a U-Haul. Mary recognized the car as Min's. Ah. Well, then. Mary knew what was happening. Today was the day Min returned to Camden Falls with her two granddaughters. Mary shook her head. Sad, those little girls. Losing their parents at such a young age. Hard on Min, too. She had lost her daughter. And now, long after raising her own two girls, she had two more to raise.

Mary stood, straightened her skirt, which was really much too heavy for this warm day, and resettled herself on the bench. She fingered the gold necklace she always wore and let her eyes wander up and down Main Street. It was a quiet afternoon in town, not many people about. Mary's gaze took in Cover to Cover, one of the bookstores, and Zack's, the hardware store with the old wooden floor full of knotholes that the smaller children in town liked to peer through, hoping to see into the basement below. There was Fig Tree, the best restaurant in Camden Falls. Mary had never eaten there, but sometimes on her way to Needle and Thread she paused to read the menu that was displayed in the glass case outside the door. There was Frank's Beans, the new coffee shop. There were the library, the post office, the real estate agency, and Dr. Malone's dental office. Mary considered Sonny's slow progress along the sidewalk as he passed Camden Falls Art Supply, then College Pizza, then Verbeyst's, the dry cleaner (which everyone except the Verbeysts mispronounced as Very Best), and finally Dutch Haus, the ice-cream parlor.

Camden Falls, population 14,672, was an old New England town. Not old by, say, European standards, but old for a town in the United States. It was about to celebrate its 350th birthday. Signs announcing the celebration, which would take place the next spring, had already been posted up and down Main Street. There were to be exhibits, a play, a parade, a carnival, fireworks. It all sounded very grand and exciting. Mary knew she would probably not be part of any of it.

Mary watched as Min Read's car approached. It slowed to a stop across the street from Needle and Thread.

"'Afternoon, Mary!" called Min, waving from her window.

"'Afternoon, Min," replied Mary.

"Slow day?" asked Min.

Mary nodded. Then she added, "Welcome back."

"Thank you. I'll see you next week."

The car continued down Main Street.

Almost home, Mary thought as she watched the car. Min and her granddaughters were almost home. Left off of Main Street, then right on Aiken Avenue, a wide street shaded by huge old maples and oaks and elms. Most of the houses on Aiken were Victorians and colonials, but one block on the west side of the street — the block on which Min and her neighbors lived — was occupied by a row of eight attached houses, one long building three stories high, built in 1882. They were the only homes of their kind in Camden Falls, and everyone referred to them simply as the Row Houses.

The fourth house from the left, between the Malones' and the Walters', was the house belonging to Min Read, which was about to become the new home of Flora and Ruby Northrop.

Mary Woolsey glanced up and down Main Street once more. She tsked at the sight of Nikki Sherman in her dirty, threadbare T-shirt, peering into Cover to Cover. Then Mary opened the door to Needle and Thread. It was time to collect her mending and go home.

CHAPTER 3

Aiken Avenue

When Flora was a very little girl visiting Camden Falls with her parents, she used to like to stand across the street from the Row Houses, squint her eyes, and pretend that instead of eight houses they were really one huge house, a giant's house an entire block long, an enormous granite mansion. Flora remembered this now as Min's car turned onto Aiken Avenue, remembered, too, that there had been a time when she wasn't sure which front door was Min's unless she counted. One — the Morrises', two — the Willets', three — the Malones', then Min's — that was number four, then Olivia's — five. Mr. Pennington's was six, the Edwardses' was seven, and number eight belonged to the Fongs. Eight doors. And eight houses all in a row, attached, identical in size, similar in layout, but otherwise nothing alike.

Running behind the gardens of the Row Houses was an alley. It gave access to the backs of the houses and to the garages, each of which sat behind its house, a narrow yard between. Most of the Row House residents parked in their garages and entered their homes through the back doors. But sometimes they parked on the street in front. Min did that now, grateful to find no traffic on Aiken and almost no cars in front of the Row Houses. She had to cross the street and park headed in the wrong direction, but she didn't think anyone would mind. Carefully, she aligned the back of the U-Haul with her front door.

"There," she said briskly. "That should make unloading easier."

Behind her, Flora and Ruby glanced at each other once more, then unclasped their hands and scooted toward the door Min was now holding open for them.

"Is King in his carrier?" asked Min. "Make sure he's safely in the carrier before you get out."

"I need King's box of supplies," said Flora. "We have to bring that in first."

The girls were fussing with King Comma, and Min was reaching in the front seat for Daisy Dear, her mind on the business of unloading the U-Haul, when Ruby exclaimed, "Hey, look!" and pointed to Min's house.

Min turned around and Flora scrambled out of the car. Draped over the front door was a banner with the word WELCOME painted on it in splashes of red.

Flora had just opened her mouth to say "I wonder who made that," when up and down the Row Houses doors began to open and people rushed outside toward Min's car.

Mr. Pennington, smiling widely, stumped along the sidewalk with his cane and wrapped his arms first around Min, then around Flora, and finally around Ruby. "I'm so glad you're back," he said. His voice always made Flora think of a wide river running slowly and smoothly.

Olivia, followed by her brothers and her parents, bounced across the front lawn to Flora and Ruby. "Hi!" she called. "Hi! You're here! And here for good, not just for a visit."

Olivia Walter, whose grandmother owned and ran Needle and Thread with Min, had grown up in the Row Houses, and she and Flora and Ruby had played together every time the Northrops had visited Camden Falls. Olivia was a full year younger than Flora (in fact, she hadn't yet turned ten), but because she had skipped second grade, she and Flora would both be in sixth grade in the fall. Olivia, Flora thought, was the bounciest, chattiest, smartest person she had ever met. Her mind was always working. Often it was organizing something, usually something to do with science. Olivia's collections — from leaves to bird's nests to butterfly wings (Olivia refused to capture and kill live butterflies) — were many. And to most of her year-older classmates they were overwhelming. As was Olivia. But Flora and Ruby thought she was wonderful and had looked forward to seeing her on every one of their visits. Olivia had looked forward to seeing them, too. In school she felt like a fish out of water. But not around Ruby and Flora.

Now tiny, wiry Olivia, wild hair flying, threw herself at Flora and Ruby, and the girls hugged fiercely. Olivia's parents hugged Min, while Henry and Jack, Olivia's younger brothers, stood back, awkward amidst the hugging.

From one end of the Row Houses, young Mr. and Mrs. Fong, artists who were new to Camden Falls, walked hand in hand toward their neighbors, followed by their corgi-mix puppies.

From the other end of the Row Houses, the four Morris children, voices at high volume, screeched down the sidewalk. "Did you see the banner?" cried Lacey, who was eight and felt quite grown up.

"We all helped make it," added Mathias, her twin.

"I helped the most," said Alyssa, the youngest Morris, who was four.

"Did not," said Travis. Travis was six but wished to be much older.

"Did too."

"Did not."

"Kids — cut it out," ordered their father.

And their mother, turning to Flora and Ruby and Min, added, "Welcome home."

This isn't my home, Flora couldn't help thinking. Everyone is being so nice, but this isn't my home.

Flora was surrounded. Lydia and Margaret Malone and their father, Dr. Malone, the dentist, were standing before her with the Willets. Flora noticed that old Mrs. Willet looked more frail than ever and was gripping her husband's hand. Mrs. Edwards, holding out a pan covered with foil, joined the crowd followed by her husband and her son, Robby, who was probably at least sixteen now.

Robby bounced up and down on his tiptoes and clapped his hands. "You know what's in the pan?" he asked. "You know what's in it? Guess what's in it, Ruby. You're Ruby, right? And you're Flora? Okay, guess what's in the pan. Guess."

"Robby, settle down," said Mr. Edwards gently.

"It's brownies!" Robby exclaimed, as if he hadn't heard his father. He clapped his hands again, fast, fingertips neatly aligned. "And I helped make them." Robby's wide face, sometimes expressionless, was now lit by a grin. Then, abruptly, he stopped smiling, and he stared into Flora's eyes, his tongue protruding wetly. "Are you sad?" he asked her loudly. "Are you sad about your parents?"

"Robby," his mother admonished him.

"Are *you* sad?" he asked Ruby.

Olivia stepped in front of Robby then, took Ruby and Flora by their elbows, and pulled them along Min's front walk. "Guess what I found today," she said. "A feather from a male cardinal. I'm pretty sure that's what it is. I have to look it up, but it's red and beautiful, and I don't have one in my feather collection."

Flora listened to the voices around her. And she thought about Robby's question. Was she sad? Well, yes. Of course she was sad. The strange thing, though, was that at the moment she didn't *feel* particularly sad. Or angry or crabby or nervous. In the car, riding along with Min and Ruby and King Comma and Daisy Dear, she had felt all those things. But as she stepped into her new life, she felt only a numb determination. She would now, as she had once heard Min say, soldier on.

She turned her attention back to all the voices.

"Robby," Mr. Edwards was saying, "remember our talk about privacy? Sometimes feelings are private, too."

"Dad, can I go back into town?" That was Lydia Malone.

"Not yet," replied her father. "We're all going to help out a bit here first."

"Bill, I *told* you — it's almost nighttime. Let's go home now." Mary Lou Willet tugged at her husband's hand, and Flora, confused because it wasn't even three o'clock in the afternoon, turned around in time to see

Mr. Willet put his arm around Mrs. Willet's thin shoulders and kiss her gently on her forehead.

Olivia's father separated himself from the crowd then and said, "Come on, everyone. Let's open the trailer and get this job done."

"King!" Ruby exclaimed, and made a dash back to the car.

The next hour went by in a blur. Flora and Ruby brought King and his things inside, and Ruby set up his litter box and showed him where it was.

"Do you think he's going to be okay?" asked Ruby. "I know he's visited here before, but this is different."

"Just don't let him outside," said Flora. "He's never been outside Min's house."

"Everybody!" shouted Ruby, standing on a stool. "Don't let our cat out! He'll be scared and confused." Hardly anyone heard her. People kept coming and going, and the front door kept opening and closing. Ruby felt a little scared and confused herself. She stepped into the bathroom for a few minutes, even though she didn't need to use it.

On the other side of the bathroom door, Flora watched as Mr. Fong and Dr. Malone carried Ruby's dresser inside.

"Which room is Ruby's?" asked Dr. Malone.

"I'll show you," said Flora.

She led the men — her new neighbors — up the wide, curving staircase to the second floor and to the first door on the right. This had been a guest room, but on their last trip to Camden Falls, when Min had insisted that the girls make the final decisions about their bedrooms, Ruby had selected this one: Ruby thought it was the coziest of the spare rooms, so she and Flora and Min had cleared it out. The room across the hall, which Min had used as a study, was to be Flora's room.

Flora returned to the stairs. "This is chaos," she had once heard her father say as he surveyed the Northrops' living room on Christmas afternoon — a sea of wrapping paper, ribbons, drying pine needles, dolls, boxes of chocolates, and torn catnip toys. Now Min's tidy house was chaos, but for a much less happy reason.

Flora paused halfway down the stairs. Below her, Ruby, who had left the bathroom, was screeching, "Don't let King out!" Three neighbors, one after the other, lugged large cardboard cartons through the door. They were followed by Lydia Malone carrying one of Flora's suitcases. "*Now* can I go?" she asked her father. Daisy Dear charged through the living room, pausing only to lick Travis's leg, which caused Travis to shriek. Mrs. Morris, Alyssa on her hip, emerged from Min's kitchen, saying, "Your refrigerator is full of food. Paula and I saw to that." Min hugged her. "Thank you. Thank you, too, Paula," she said, turning to Robby's mother, then added, "What would I do without all of you?"

Flora made her way down the rest of the stairs,

squeezing to the side to make room for Mr. Walter, Olivia's father, who was carrying a rocking chair in the other direction. At the bottom, she met Olivia.

"I think the trailer's almost empty," said Olivia. "People are starting to go home."

"It *is* empty," said Ruby. She deposited King in the living room. "What's Min going to do with it now?"

"My dad's going to return it to the U-Haul place for her," replied Olivia.

"Your dad is? That's nice of him," said Ruby.

"We're all kind of like one big family," Olivia said.

Ruby looked around at the neighbors. "A colorful family," she said.

Olivia grinned. "We *are* pretty colorful."

When the Row Houses had been built, the first families to occupy them were white. All white. The help — the people for whom the maids' rooms and butlers' pantries had been created — had been white, too. Mr. Pennington was the first person of color to move into one of the Row Houses. That was decades ago when his wife was still alive, and Camden Falls had buzzed about the event for more than two years. But these days, as Ruby had pointed out, the Row House neighbors were pretty colorful, and no one thought much about it. Olivia and her family, Mr. Pennington (more than eighty years old now), and the Morrises were African-American. The Fongs were Asian-American, and the Malones, the Willets, the Edwardses, and Min and Flora and Ruby were Caucasian. Light skin, dark skin, brown eyes, blue eyes, green eyes, red hair, black hair, brown hair, blond hair — a human rainbow had swarmed through Ruby's new home that afternoon.

The front door banged open again, and Mr. Edwards stepped inside and called to no one in particular, "That's the last of it."

"My stars and garters," replied Min, following him through the door. "I can't believe it. Is everything in your rooms, girls?"

"Yup," replied Ruby.

Min sank into a chair in the living room and realized that except for Mr. Edwards and Olivia and her father, the neighbors had drifted away.

"You want to come upstairs with us?" Ruby asked Olivia.

"Sure. I can help you organize your rooms," replied Olivia, who liked nothing better than putting things in order.

"Don't feel you have to do all the unpacking today, girls," Min called after them.

In the second-floor hallway, Ruby stood outside her room, Flora stood outside hers, and Olivia stood between them, glancing from one room to the other.

Flora felt a tightening in her chest, in her throat, and knew that tears were threatening. She swallowed them. And then a phrase jumped into her mind. The Point of No Return. Flora saw it as if it were a weathered sign nailed to a tree, as if she were a character in a book and she had walked and walked through a dense and scary forest and now, suddenly, had reached The Point of No Return.

In the car, on the endless trip to Camden Falls, Flora could have said (and nearly had said), "Min, please just turn the car around and take us back home." But now Flora and Ruby had arrived in Camden Falls and the trailer had been unloaded and their furniture had been carried all the way upstairs and the helpful neighbors had left and there was no going back.

Flora looked at Ruby and saw that her eyes had filled with tears, too, and also that her lower lip was quivering. This was a sure sign that a full-blown wail was not far away.

Flora looked at Olivia and saw that Olivia was looking at both of them. In a flash, Olivia went into action. "Wow," she said, "your rooms are a *really* big mess. Okay. Here's what we should do. First, put all the furniture exactly where you want it. Then stack the boxes neatly in the middle of the room. After that, put your clothes away. Last of all, unpack the boxes."

Flora couldn't help but smile.

"Are you a moving expert?" asked Ruby seriously, her lower lip now still.

"Nope," said Olivia. "I just like to organize stuff. You know that."

The girls moved the furniture around, and Ruby

and Flora were arranging their clothes in cedar wardrobes (the Row Houses, like many older homes, had almost no closets) when the doorbell rang.

Ruby could hear Min talking on the phone, so she yelled, "I'll get it!" and ran down the stairs. She opened the front door to find Robby Edwards standing on the stoop, holding a squirming cat.

"King Comma!" exclaimed Ruby. She held the door open as Robby stepped inside and set King on the floor.

"I saw the kitty in my backyard," said Robby, "and I said to him, 'You are in the wrong yard, kitty,' and then I brought him over here."

"Wow. Thank you," replied Ruby. "I don't know how he got out."

Robby stared at her. "Why is his name King Comma?" he asked.

Ruby looked at the big cat. He was mostly black, but his paws were white, as if they had been dipped in milk, and there was a white patch on his chest and a white mark between his eyes. "Do you know what a comma is?" asked Ruby.

Robby frowned. "Yes," he said finally. "A comma is what I put after 'Dear Ruby' in a *friendly* letter. Which is what I would write to you, if I wrote you a letter."

"Right," said Ruby. "Okay. See that mark on his forehead? It's shaped like a comma. And when Flora and I named him, we added King because we think he's royal."

Robby studied King Comma. "You could have named him King Boots," he said. "Okay. I have to go. It's the rule. Good-bye."

Robby let himself out of the house, and Ruby turned around to find Olivia and Flora halfway down the stairs. "What is it that Robby has?" she asked Olivia. "I forget what it's called."

"Down syndrome," replied Olivia. She checked her watch. "I'd better go home. I'll see you tomorrow."

Later, when Olivia had gone home and Ruby was in her room, engaged in a search for her tap shoes, Flora sat on her bed, alone for the first time that day. From downstairs she could hear Min banging around in the kitchen. From across the hall she could hear Ruby ripping open packing cartons. Flora let out a sigh of monumental proportions, then turned to her own cartons. ART SUPPLIES, one was labeled. BOOKS. FABRIC. Flora tiptoed across the room, quietly closed the door, returned to her bed, and thought of her old house, her old neighborhood, her old school, and Annika and her old friends. She missed them all. But most of all she missed her parents.

Flora wanted to go home.

CHAPTER 4

King's Adventure

The next day, Sunday, dawned bright and sunny and already hot. In the garden behind Min's Row House, the iris plants were in bloom, tall spiky stalks with deep purple blossoms. A timid phoebe, her nest hidden nearby, perched on the branch of a dogwood tree, waving her tail feathers. The air smelled of blooms and sunshine and damp earth and leaves that were still new.

Ruby surveyed this from the window of the dining room, where Min had set the table for breakfast. Then she turned to face Min and Flora, crossed her arms, and said, "Why are we eating in here?"

"In the dining room?" said Min. "I just thought it would be nice to have a fancy breakfast on your first morning in Camden Falls."

Ruby's eyes took in the plate of bacon, the dish of scrambled eggs, the toast, the orange juice, Min's pot of coffee. "I hate eggs," she said, and stomped out of the room.

"Good night, nurse," murmured Min, which made Flora smile. She didn't know what all of Min's expressions meant, but she liked hearing them.

"What's wrong with *her*?" Flora asked, feeling much better after a long and dreamless sleep.

"Just crabby," replied Min. "You know Ruby."

Flora nodded. When Flora was sad, she grew quiet. When Ruby was sad, she got crabby.

Min and Flora ate breakfast with Daisy, who sat by Min's chair, resting her golden chin on Min's knee and following every forkful of food with pitiful brown eyes.

"You look tragic, Daisy Dear," said Min. "Truly tragic. No one would ever know you ate your own breakfast not ten minutes ago."

Flora and Min dawdled and chatted, and Min drank three cups of coffee. After breakfast, when the dishes had been cleared and Min had opened all the windows on the first floor in order to let in the soft summer smells, Flora went upstairs to tackle the boxes piled by her bed. She glanced into Ruby's room. King Comma was curled up in an armchair, and Ruby, wearing a tutu, a tiara, and her tap shoes, was arranging china animals on her dresser. She looked quite cheerful.

"I'm changing the goat's name from Jennifer to Pilar," she announced, and Flora just stared at her. The china animals, most of them, had been given to Ruby by their parents, who had picked them up on trips or in gift shops. Ruby treated each one as a member of her family, assigning them names and personalities and histories. How, Flora wondered now, could Ruby look at them and see them only as animals, instead of as gifts from their parents? Where was Ruby's heart? But then Flora remembered Ruby's earlier bad mood, so she said nothing, stepping into her own room and closing the door behind her.

Two hours later, with help from Min, who had Sundays off from Needle and Thread, most of the unpacking had been finished. The former guest room and the former study now looked like bedrooms.

"Let's take a break," said Min, and at that moment, the doorbell rang.

Flora and Ruby dashed down the stairs.

"Maybe it's Olivia!" said Flora, but when she opened the door, she found Robby on the stoop.

"Hi, Flora. Hi, Ruby," said Robby, and before Flora could close the door, King slipped between her feet, shot outside, and hurtled across the lawn and into the Malones' yard.

"Hey!" shouted Ruby.

"Help!" cried Robby.

"Min, King's out again!" Flora called.

"Oh, dear," said Min as she hurried downstairs.

"Chase him!" said Ruby.

Ruby, Flora, and Robby ran across the Malones' lawn and into the Willets' yard, calling, "King! King Comma! Come here, King!" But he was already out of sight.

Margaret Malone poked her head around her front door. "What's wrong?" she asked.

"Our cat got out," said Flora, panting.

"Your cat's gone?" said Mr. Willet through his screen door.

"Yes," said Ruby. "King Comma."

"I can't leave Mary Lou right now," said Mr. Willet, "but I'll be on the lookout."

"Hey, Flora! Ruby!" someone called, and Flora turned around to see Olivia running along the sidewalk. Behind her were Robby's mother and Mrs. Fong.

"Olivia, King's gone!" cried Flora. "He just got out a minute ago, but we can't see him anywhere."

"Okay," said Olivia. She thought for a moment, then straightened up as tall as she was able and put her hand on her hip. "All right. Cats are fast. Everybody, spread out! Look in trees and under bushes." She pointed to Ruby and Robby. "Ruby, you and Robby go get my brothers and the Morris kids. Tell them to look in the backyards and the garages. The grown-ups should look in the front yards and across the street. Flora, you come with me."

"Where are we going?" asked Flora, who felt breathless just listening to Olivia.

"Around. We'd better fan out farther."

"Town is only two blocks away," said Flora. "What if he's in *town*? He'll get killed there. It's a busy street."

"It's not *that* busy," said Olivia. "Don't worry yet. Just come on."

Flora and Olivia hurried down Aiken Avenue, calling, "King! King! King Comma!"

They passed old New England homes set on wide lawns. They saw stones houses and saltbox houses and several houses that Flora knew her mother would have called gingerbread, with curlicues and fancy trim, painted bright colors. But no King.

"This is just terrible," said Flora, blinking back tears. "King has no idea where he is. What if he doesn't come back? Did you ever read that book *The Incredible Journey*? About those pets who traveled across the country — I think it was across the country — to find their owners? Or what about all those stories about cats and dogs who walk hundreds of miles back to their old homes? What if King is already trying to find his way back to *our* old home?"

"Flora, stop worrying," said Olivia briskly as she wound through town. "I don't think anything that dramatic is going to happen. Plus, you and Ruby are King's owners and you're right here. King won't want to leave you. He's probably just out exploring his new territory. I have a good feeling someone's going to find him soon." Olivia paused. She lowered her voice. "Hey, look where we are."

Flora's eyes followed Olivia's pointing finger to one of the strangest and loveliest homes she had ever seen.

"What is that place?" she whispered.

"It's Mary Woolsey's house."

Flora let her gaze linger on the yard. There was no grass in it, not even a teeny patch of lawn. Instead, the house was surrounded by nothing but gardens — gardens that meandered to the edges of the property and back to the walls of the house, and didn't even stop there. From behind rosebushes and ferns and bleeding hearts, ivy and clematis twined up the house, covering every inch of it except the windows and the door.

"It's . . . beautiful," said Flora.

The gardens were lush and well tended. Everywhere she looked, Flora could see things in bloom — familiar flowers, plus lots of things she couldn't identify. Yellows and pinks and reds and purples and blues, tall flowers and spiky flowers and delicate flowers and flowers with huge blossoms, flowers trailing and drooping and climbing. Neat brick paths wound through the gardens, and here and there a bench or a birdbath had been placed. Butterflies drifted from bloom to bloom, and Flora saw a hummingbird gathering nectar from a fuchsia blossom.

The house nestled in the midst of these gardens was tiny, reminding Flora of a fairy cottage she had once seen in a picture book. One door, a window on either side of it, a low sloping roof. Flora guessed there were no more than four rooms inside.

"Who's Mary Woolsey?" asked Flora.

"Mary Woolsey," Olivia replied, her voice still low, "is a crazy woman. We call her Scary Mary. She lives here and she almost never comes out, except to go to Needle and Thread."

"Needle and Thread!" Flora cried, then clapped her hand over her mouth. "You're kidding me, Olivia. Aren't you?" she said more softly. "You're just trying to scare me. She doesn't go to Needle and Thread."

"Yes, she does. This is all true. Mary Woolsey has lived in this very house all her life, and she's about eighty years old. She lives alone. She's a . . . what do you call it when you hardly ever leave your home?"

"A recluse?"

"Yes, a recluse. She only leaves three times a week to go shopping and then to Needle and Thread. That's how she earns her money. At our store. She takes in mending and stuff. People drop off their sewing for her, and she brings most of it to her house, does the work, and returns it to the store. Then the people come and pick up their things."

"Min and your grandmother let her do that?" asked Flora.

"It was Min and Gigi's idea." (Gigi was what Olivia called her grandmother, Mrs. Walter.)

Flora was now standing still, trying to see into the windows of Scary Mary's house.

"Don't stare!" hissed Olivia.

Flora took a step back. "Why is she so scary?" she asked. "What's wrong with her?"

"She's just crazy, that's all. Has been forever and ever. Some people say she has stuff buried in those gardens, and only she knows where to find it."

"What kind of stuff?"

"I don't know. Treasure. And other people say she has someone — a child, maybe — hidden in her house. In the basement, I think."

Flora shivered. Then she let out a small screech. "I think I see her in the window!"

Olivia grabbed Flora's hand. "Come on!" she cried.

The girls turned and ran back to Aiken Avenue. When they reached the Row Houses, they were panting. They leaned over, hands on knees, gulping air.

They were just catching their breath when Ruby found them and said, "No sign of King yet."

"Oh, no." Flora straightened up. The Row House neighbors were still milling around, calling and searching.

"All right. We'd better go into town then," said Olivia. "We can go to the stores on Main Street — the ones that are open — and tell the owners to watch for King."

"I'm coming with you," said Ruby.

Main Street was busier than Flora had expected it would be.

"Church just let out," Olivia informed her. "After church, people stay in town for lunch or to run errands."

Ruby, trailing behind Flora and Olivia as they made their way along Main Street, looked in the shops they passed. She saw the ice-cream parlor that was called Dutch Haus and the dry cleaner that was called something like Very Best. They were closed, but next door was College Pizza, and that was open. Olivia poked her head inside and called to the woman behind the counter, "Hi, Beth! We're looking for a lost cat. He's black and white and his name is King. If you see him, would you call my grandmother? Or Flora and Ruby's? Their grandmother is Mrs. Read."

"Oh! You're the new girls," said Beth. "Welcome to Camden Falls."

"Thank you," said Flora and Ruby.

As they were leaving, Ruby caught sight of a familiar-looking girl seated at a booth with two boys and another girl. Ruby tugged Olivia's shirt. "Doesn't she live next door to Min?" she asked.

Olivia glanced at the booth, then hustled Ruby and Flora outside. "Yes," she said. "That's Lydia Malone. She's Margaret's younger sister. But don't talk to her when you see her with her friends. She used to be nice, but now she isn't, *especially* when she's with those friends."

"They don't look very nice, either," said Flora.

"They aren't," replied Olivia.

Olivia and Ruby and Flora continued their way up and down Main Street, poking their heads in Ma Grand-mère, a bakery, and Cover to Cover, a bookstore. They met a very cranky woman who owned a shop called Stuff 'n' Nonsense. And everywhere they went, Olivia told people about King.

By the time they returned to Aiken Avenue and the Row Houses, Flora was exhausted and had almost given up on finding King Comma. So she was honestly surprised to be greeted by a very cheerful Robby, who ran down the sidewalk toward them, saying, "Guess what! We found King Comma. We found him way up high in Mr. Pennington's garage. Mr. Morris got him down, and now he's back at your house."

Flora was so relieved that she threw her arms around Robby and thanked him six times. She didn't know what she would have done if King had been lost forever. Then she took Olivia by one hand and Ruby by the other, and the girls ran to Min's house, Flora calling, "King! We're back!" as they pushed through the door.

CHAPTER 5

A Peek in the Windows

When the Row Houses were built, which was more than fifty years before Min was born, they were some of the grandest homes in Camden Falls. Each was three stories high, topped off by an attic accessible by a ladder that dropped down into a hallway below. On the first floor were a large kitchen, a butler's pantry, a dining room, and a living room. On the second floor were four bedrooms. And on the third floor were several smaller rooms, the sleeping quarters for maids. In 1882, the wealthy people who lived in the Row Houses all had maids who slept in the maids' quarters, and butlers who used the butlers' pantries. But now, 125 years later, while the Row Houses were still grand, the people who lived in them did not have maids and butlers, or chauffeurs and gardeners, for that matter. Many of the butlers' pantries had been turned into breakfast nooks or mudrooms, and the rooms in the maids' quarters were nurseries or playrooms or offices or dens or guest rooms. The backyards, which once boasted formal gardens, were now cluttered with basketball hoops and vegetable plots, jungle gyms and storage sheds and swing sets. Even Min's yard, with her carefully tended flower beds, was home to a tire swing and a tree fort that Flora and Ruby's mother had played with when she was their age. The twelve children who lived in the Row Houses these days (twelve if you counted Lydia, Margaret, and Robby, who were teenagers and did not consider themselves children) ran freely through the eight yards and in and out of the houses, comfortable with each of their neighbors, old and young.

Now, if you were walking north along Aiken Avenue and came to the Row Houses on a warm Sunday evening in June, you would find most of the windows open to let in the summer air. And if you paused on the sidewalk, you might be able to take a peek in the windows and glimpse the lives of the people inside. In the house on the left end, you would find the Morris family, Elise and Paul, their four children, Lacey, Mathias, Travis, and Alyssa, and their hamsters and guinea pig. Supper is long over — the Morrises eat early — and Alyssa and Travis are already in their pajamas. Mrs. Morris is commenting to her husband that the children are growing up so fast. This fall Alyssa, who's the youngest, will be in all-day preschool, and what will Mrs. Morris do with herself while the children are gone?

In the next house you would find Bill and Mary Lou Willet. They're nearly seventy-eight years old, both of them. Their birthdays are just a week apart in August. Mr. Willet is encouraging his wife to change out of her clothes and into her nightgown, but she won't. She's been wearing these same clothes for four days and four nights now, and Mr. Willet can't convince her to put on anything else. He can't convince her to take a shower, either, or to comb her hair or take her pills or brush her teeth.

"Come on, honey," he says. "You'll feel so much better in a nice clean nightgown. Trust me."

But his wife, who's patting their cat, Sweetie, replies, "You know, my sister was here again today and we had such a pleasant conversation."

Mrs. Willet's sister has been dead for more than twenty years.

Next door to the Willets are the Malones. There's Margaret, sixteen now, drinking tea with her father, Dr. Malone, the dentist. They're sitting at the kitchen table, their cats, Twinkle and Bandit, nearby, and Dr. Malone is laughing at something Margaret has said. Upstairs, Lydia, who's fourteen, has shut herself in her bedroom and is sitting before her computer, instant messaging her friends. When her father calls upstairs to her, she ignores him.

The house to the north of the Malones' is Min's. She was born in that house — she was Mindy Davis then — and has lived there for most of her life, first as a child with her parents and her brother and sister, later as a wife and mother, and now as a grandmother. On this evening, Min, Flora, Ruby, Daisy Dear, and King Comma are in the kitchen and Min is making dinner. Daisy and King are lying on the floor just inches apart, and this is one of the first times they have been so close to each other without growling.

"They're finally getting along," Ruby whispers, not wanting to break the spell. Then she adds, still whispering, "Min, is there a dance school in Camden Falls?"

Next door in Olivia's house, Mr. Walter closes up his home office on the third floor and leaves his computer and papers behind. He finds Olivia, her younger brothers, Henry and Jack, and his wife playing Clue on the living room floor. Olivia looks up when her father enters the room and thinks he looks not only tired but discouraged.

In the next house is Mr. Pennington. He's eighty-two years old, and Jacques, his cocker spaniel, is nearly as old in dog years. Mr. Pennington is peering in Jacques's food dish, seeing lots of kibble there and trying to remember if it's old kibble or new kibble.

In the seventh house, the house belonging to the Edwards family, Robby and his parents are lingering over dessert, and Robby is talking about his beloved day camp.

"When does it start, Mom?" he asks.

"In two weeks," replies his mother.

Robby is grinning. "Swimming in the pool!" he says. "Basketball, nature walks, arts and crafts, swimming in the pool, snacktime when we make our own snacks. That's what I like best. Making our own snacks. Except for swimming in the pool."

In the last house, the one at the right end, live Mr. and Mrs. Fong, artists who make furniture and jewelry. They have a studio in town, where they work and sell their pieces. At home they have turned the small rooms on the third floor into a second studio, and this evening they are there, working side by side, their puppies resting in the doorway.

Now walk back to the fourth house, to Min's, and take one last peek in the windows. Min is almost finished making dinner, and Flora is tossing a salad. It's Ruby's job to set the table.

"Let's use the good china," says Ruby. "I know where it is. We can have a fancy dinner tonight."

You would never guess, from a quick peek in Min's window, that she and Ruby and Flora have been a family for just five months.

CHAPTER 6

Needle and Thread

On Monday morning, Sonny Sutphin, making his way slowly through town in his wheelchair, noticed Min Read walking smartly along Main Street, hand in hand with her granddaughters.

"'Morning, Min," called Sonny.

"'Morning, Sonny," replied Min. "Sonny, I don't believe you've met my grandchildren yet. This is Flora Northrop and this is Ruby Northrop." Flora and Ruby stepped forward and shook Sonny's hand.

"Pleased to meet you," said Sonny. He turned to Min. "Back at work?"

"My first day. I've been away for a long time. Ruby and Flora are coming to the store with me."

"We're going to spend *every day* there," said Ruby, glaring at Min and stabbing the toe of her sneaker into a crack in the sidewalk.

"Ruby," said Min, a warning in her voice.

"Well, what am I going to *do* all day?"

"At Needle and Thread? Goodness me, I think you'll keep yourself occupied," replied Min. "And please don't whine. It isn't becoming."

Ruby almost said "Becoming what?" but stopped herself in time.

Sonny waved good-bye, and Min and Ruby and Flora continued down the street. Ruby was scowling fiercely, but Flora wore a small smile on her face. Flora hadn't admitted this to her sister — it wasn't any fun telling something good to someone crabby — but she was looking forward to spending her days at Needle and Thread. In fact, just thinking about this was one of the few things that made her feel truly happy. Needlework was Flora's passion. She liked sewing. She liked quilting. She liked embroidering. She liked embellishing things. She liked fabric and buttons and beads and patterns and ribbons and lace. (She also liked knitting and crafting and card making, but Needle and Thread didn't carry many supplies for those hobbies.)

When Flora was very small, her busy grandmother had taken the time during visits to teach her to sew. (Later, Min had offered to teach Ruby, but Ruby was more interested in ballet classes and tap routines and voice lessons.) Flora had first made pillows and blankets for her dolls but was soon learning crewel work and even smocking. Her mother had taught her to knit.

And now the thought of spending summer days at Needle and Thread made her let go of Min's hand and skip the last few paces to the store.

"Mrs. Walter's already here!" she said, peering through the door.

From behind her, Ruby said, "Do we really have to spend *every single day* here, Min?"

Min stopped walking. She looked down at her granddaughter. "Ruby," she said, trying to sound patient, "this is my store. Mrs. Walter and I own it. We have to run it. Do you understand that?" (Ruby nodded.) "I have worked out the best hours I can, but I still have to be here at least five days a week. In the fall you will go to school, and if you want to go to after-school activities you may. But this is the summertime. What do you suggest you do all day while I'm at the store? I can't leave you at home alone, and I haven't arranged for a baby-sitter —"

"I don't *want* a baby-sitter. I'm not a baby."

"Okay. And I'm sorry, but I didn't get around to looking into day camp or anything else. This has been a busy time. I know it isn't what you want, but bear with me. We all have to make sacrifices. I promise you, though, things will work out. For now, you and Flora will come to the store with me. I don't think you're going to be bored. There will be plenty for you to do. Please just give it a try. I'm doing the best I can."

"Okay," muttered Ruby. "I'll try."

"Thank you," said Min.

Flora flung open the door to Needle and Thread. She was greeted by the smell of coffee, and while the coffeemaker steamed and gurgled, Olivia's grandmother was setting out cups and spoons and packets of sugar on a table at the front of the store.

"Hi, Mrs. Walter!" said Flora.

"Flora," Mrs. Walter replied warmly. She wrapped Flora in a giant, bosomy hug. "How are you?"

"Fine, thank you," said Flora.

Ruby and Min stepped inside then, and Mrs. Walter opened her arms to Ruby. "I'm glad you're here," she said.

Min grinned at Mrs. Walter. "Ruby wants to be put to work," she said. "She's afraid she's going to be bored."

"Bored? Never," said Mrs. Walter.

Flora turned her attention away from crabby Ruby and looked around the store. She let out a long, satisfied sigh. There in the front of Needle and Thread were the couches for people who stopped by for a chat-and-stitch. All day long, Min and Mrs. Walter's customers dropped in with their sewing projects and sat on the couches, drinking coffee or tea, sewing and chatting with whomever else was there. The coffeepot was kept going all day long, and often people brought in cookies or muffins to share.

"See? Isn't this nice?" Flora said to Ruby. "People will be coming in for chat-and-stitches."

"And sometimes," said Mrs. Walter, "we have a special event here in the evening — a lecture, or an author reading from a new book."

"Lectures and books about sewing?" asked Ruby.

"Not necessarily," replied Mrs. Walter. "Needle and Thread is a gathering place. All sorts of things go on here."

Flora drifted toward the back of the store, past the checkout counter and several racks lined with bolts of fabric, to the tables where classes were held. There were classes for adults and for kids. All kinds of classes. Quilting, ribbon embroidery, holiday projects.

"Min?" Flora called to the front of the store. "Could I please take a kids' class sometime?"

"I think you could help *teach* the kids' classes," replied Min, and Flora smiled and looked at her shoes. She continued wandering through the store, stopping to examine the cards of buttons on the spinner racks, the tables where customers could look through pattern books, the counter where fabric was cut, and the arrays of laces and ribbons and zippers and notions and thread and interfacing and needlework magazines.

"What's that table for?" Flora asked Mrs. Walter. She had passed a display of sewing machines and come upon a messy table, piled with fabric, patterns, and articles of clothing, each with a receipt attached.

"That's where Miss Woolsey works. She comes in several times a week to take in mending and altering, or to do custom sewing. She does some of her work here and the rest at home."

"Miss Woolsey?" repeated Flora, her voice rising to a squeak. "Do you mean Sca — Mary Woolsey?"

"I do," replied Mrs. Walter in a voice that stopped Flora from asking any more questions. "She'll be in this afternoon."

And so Flora and Ruby's first day at Needle and Thread began to unfold. By nine, Liz Durbin and Rick O'Bannen, the store clerks, had arrived for work. Five minutes later, Olivia arrived.

"Is there anything I can organize?" she wanted to know, and her grandmother asked her to tidy the button racks and the rows of zippers and piping and bias tape.

"What can I do?" asked Ruby.

"I have a stack of things that came in for people who placed special orders," Min replied. "They're all right here with receipts attached. You can make sure we wrote the customers' phone numbers on the receipts. If you don't see a number, look it up in the phone book and write it on the receipt. There's the phone book."

Ruby's eyes widened. This was an important job.

Min asked Flora to start working on a sample outfit to display in the store. "We just got in all these adorable patterns for fall skirts and vests for younger girls," said

Min. "Gigi and I wanted to make up several and hang them around the store later this summer when people come in to start their back-to-school sewing. Do you think you could make a skirt and vest? I'll show you the fabric Gigi and I would like used in the display. I've already washed it."

So Flora spent the morning at a class table in the back, laying out the pieces for a corduroy skirt and a pumpkin-print vest, size six.

By lunchtime, Ruby had finished her task and was allowed to take a handful of letters to the post office and to pick up Liz's lunch order from College Pizza. Olivia had tidied everything in sight. And Flora, while she was busy with the corduroy, had also had a long and slightly confusing conversation with a haughty woman who was so dressed up that Flora thought she must be on her way to a party.

"My name is Mrs. DuVane," said the woman as she approached Flora. "Do you . . . work here?"

"Sort of. My grandmo —"

"Oh, well, that's fine then. I saw the notice in the window about the ribbon embroidery classes. I'm going to sign up, so I'll be needing ribbon, of course, but I only want *silk* ribbon."

"I'm pretty sure that's all my grandmother carries."

"Because silk is the best. I wouldn't use anything else."

"Well, the ribbon is over there, and it's all silk," said Flora, pointing. "Maybe you should ask my —"

But Mrs. DuVane had hurried away while Flora was still talking.

"Don't worry about her," said Olivia later, when Flora recounted the conversation to her. "She's just a —" Olivia caught sight of her grandmother standing nearby and said quickly, "She's fussy, that's all."

At two o'clock, when Flora was beginning to feel a bit tired, the bell over the front door jangled and in came an old woman, wearing what Flora thought was way too many clothes for the warm day. She was carrying a cloth parcel and wheezing slightly.

"'Afternoon, Mary," said Min and Mrs. Walter at the same time.

The old woman didn't reply, just raised one hand in greeting before lowering it to touch a tiny star that hung from a delicate necklace half hidden under a scarf. Then she made her way to the little table near the display of sewing machines.

Flora looked around the store and caught Olivia's eye. Olivia nodded. Here was Scary Mary. In person.

Min introduced Flora and Ruby to Mary a few minutes later and they shook her hand — Flora gingerly, and Ruby more robustly since she didn't know anything about Scary Mary yet — but Mary Woolsey barely spoke to them. She barely spoke to her customers, either, Flora realized later as she watched people bring their torn pants and too-long skirts to her. They would explain what they needed, and Mary would take some measurements, then carefully make notes on a battered notepad. She would suggest a price for the work, and the customers would agree, thank her, and leave.

Later that afternoon, Flora and Ruby, both exhausted from their first day in the store, lay down on the couches by the front door. Flora began paging through a sewing magazine. She leafed through articles on paper piecing and the perfect set-in sleeve and how to miter a corner, and then she came to a photo of a firefighter handing a teddy bear to a small boy. The title of the article was "Project Teddy: Creating Hope with Handmade Teddy Bears." The article explained that in a town not far from Seattle, a sewing store was helping children cope with grief by donating hundreds of hand-made teddies to various organizations in the area.

Flora remembered the teddy bears that had been given to her and Ruby in the hospital the night of the car accident, and an idea began to take shape.

CHAPTER 7

On the Edge

Nikki Sherman was eye to eye with a grasshopper, separated from it only by the glass jar in which she had carefully prepared a grasshopper-friendly environment. Nikki studied the grasshopper's head. Then she drew in her breath and returned to the sketch she was working on, using a bitten-up pencil and a sheet of lined notebook paper.

The afternoon was hot and still, very still. The steps on which Nikki was sitting were warm from the sun. She set down the jar and her drawing, stretched her skinny legs in front of her, and yawned. It wasn't often that her yard was this quiet. But her mother had taken Mae down the road to see the Shaws' donkey, and Tobias had gone off with friends of his, and her father — well, he could be anywhere. Nikki hadn't seen him in several days.

Nikki sat still and let her gaze take in the yard. She was aware that it was probably one of the most run-down, dirty yards in all of Camden Falls. If there was anything good about living so far from town it was that very few people passed the Shermans' place, so most of Nikki's classmates didn't know where she lived, out here, on the edge. Not that Nikki spoke much to her classmates. She saw how they looked at her, at her worn clothes, some of them hand-me-downs from Tobias, even though he was a full six years older than she, and a boy to boot. No matter how Nikki tried to keep up with the washing and the mending (on the days when her mother couldn't cope), her clothes were torn and shabby and faded and dirty.

From time to time, her classmates informed her that she smelled.

Nikki thought of the yards of the houses in town, yards with grass growing and flowers blooming and tall trees shading porches, tidy yards with maybe a jungle gym in the back or a swing hanging from the limb of a maple, but no litter or clutter or ramshackle sheds. In Nikki's yard were four wooden structures that her father had once used for storage and for workspaces, three of which were falling apart. There were also two old cars, neither with wheels; a woodpile; an ax that had been left for so long in a log that the blade had rusted; an ancient refrigerator, its door removed; a burning pile; and a heap of trash resembling a dump, which was in fact garbage that Nikki's parents had been too lazy to take to the actual dump. What wasn't in the yard was grass, unless you counted crabgrass. There were no flowers or trees, either. Just packed earth and plenty of weeds.

"*Woof!*"

Nikki smiled. Trotting across the yard was Paw-Paw, one of the many stray dogs who hung around the edges of Nikki's yard. He'd shown up in the spring and was Nikki's favorite.

"Come here, Paw-Paw," said Nikki. "It's okay. Dad isn't home. I'm the only one here."

Paw-Paw crossed the yard cautiously, glancing from side to side, but when he reached Nikki, he relaxed. He plopped down on his haunches and offered his front paw to her, something he had done the first time Nikki and Mae had seen him, which was why Mae, five years old at the time, had named him Paw-Paw.

As she often did when she talked to Paw-Paw, Nikki now said, "Who used to own you? Huh? Who did, Paw-Paw? Someone must have owned you. You're trained. And you're friendly. But if someone owned you, why did they let you go?" Nikki wished she knew the story of every single one of the stray dogs.

"Come on," said Nikki, brushing off her shorts and standing up. "I'll get you some food. It'll be okay. You can eat as much as you want, and you won't even have to hide. Now, if Dad was here . . ."

Nikki's voice trailed off. She crossed the yard to one of the sheds and grabbed the bag of kibble she had stashed there. It usually took Nikki three weeks to earn enough money to buy each bag of dog food, and she was careful to keep them hidden. The last time her father had found one of the bags he had slurrily told Nikki that if she didn't stop attracting those filthy beasts to his property he would take her outside and tan her hide. Then he had burned the bag and its contents.

Nikki hadn't worried much about the threat. Her father had been too drunk and forgetful when he'd made it (what he had actually said was that if Nikki didn't shtop trekking those filthy feasts to his proppity he would take her outshide and tan her tide), but she couldn't afford to buy extra bags of food. Not unless she found a way to earn more money, and her money-earning opportunities were few.

Nikki carried the bag to the bushes at one side of her yard and filled the bowls she left there.

"Come and get it, everybody!" she called, and from behind sheds, from under bushes, from the farthest edges of her yard crept one scruffy dog after another. Nikki hadn't named most of them; the dogs came and went. While they were there, though, Nikki did the best she could for them.

Nikki was returning the bag of kibble to the shed, her mind on the grasshopper and her sketch, when she heard the sound of tires on gravel.

Oh, no, she thought. Not Dad. Not on such a peaceful afternoon.

But the car that was crunching its way toward the Shermans' house was a red Audi in fine condition, one Tobias envied.

Nikki clapped her hand to her forehead and groaned. It was the old bat. Mrs. DuVane. Nikki would almost rather have seen her father's dented truck come roaring up the drive.

The Audi glided to a stop by the house, and as Nikki approached it, the driver's door opened and a pair of long legs, delicate sandals on the feet, slid out, followed by the rest of Mrs. DuVane.

"Nicolette! Just the person I wanted to see."

"Hi, Mrs. DuVane," said Nikki.

"I've had a wonderful idea. Come, sit on the steps with me and we'll have a chat."

Nikki followed Mrs. DuVane to the stoop, sticking out her tongue and making faces at her back. Mrs. DuVane, who years ago had attended Camden Falls Central High School with Nikki's mother, had somehow taken on Nikki and Tobias and Mae as personal charity projects. Nikki wasn't quite sure how this had come about. All she knew was that her mother was an acquaintance of Mrs. DuVane, and that Mrs. DuVane showed up periodically to take Mae shopping for school clothes (so she could hold up her head in class) or Tobias out for a fancy dinner (in order to teach him manners) or Nikki to the community theatre (to expose her to culture). Nikki knew they should be grateful for such treats, especially since Mrs. DuVane often made vague promises about helping with education — and Nikki desperately wanted to go to college someday. But it was hard to be grateful since Mrs. DuVane made Nikki and her brother and sister feel stupid and needy and awkward.

All the Shermans privately referred to her as the old bat.

When they reached the stoop, Mrs. DuVane said, "Is your mother here, Nicolette?"

Nikki shook her head. "She's out with Mae."

"All right, I'll talk to her later. Listen, I've just come from Needle and Thread. Do you know Needle and Thread? In town?"

Nikki nodded.

"Well, I've signed up to take a class in ribbon embroidery there, and I've decided that you should come with me. The class is for adults, but I'm sure the people who run the store wouldn't mind if you came along as well. I saw other little girls there today. One of them seemed to be quite an accomplished seamstress, which is a wonderful thing for a girl. Now, I know you like to draw, so I thought you'd like sewing as well."

Nikki didn't see the connection. She did like to draw. And she liked animals. She wanted to become a wildlife artist one day. What did that have to do with sewing?

"You're a very creative person," Mrs. DuVane continued. "We must nurture that. It will stand you in good stead in the future." Mrs. DuVane paused. "Is your phone working, dear?"

"Yes. We paid the bill yesterday."

"All right. Tell your mother I'll call her tonight. And I'll be picking you up in three weeks to go to Needle and Thread. In the meantime, brush up on your sewing skills. *À demain!* That's French for 'good-bye.'"

Actually, thought Nikki as Mrs. DuVane climbed back into her car, that's French for "good-bye until tomorrow."

CHAPTER 8

Trouble at the Row Houses

On a sultry July afternoon, Olivia Walter looked up from the book she was reading on one of the couches in her grandmother's store. The hot weather had kept some people at home but had driven others to Needle and Thread for a chat-and-stitch in the air-conditioning. Olivia listened to their conversation, catching phrases here and there: mini piping, pin-tuck foot, lace insert. She watched Min show a woman how to make a bullion knot.

At the back of the store, Flora was finishing up a vest and skirt set. Ruby sat beside her, wearing head-phones and singing along to *The Music Man.* "Oh, oh, the Wells Fargo wagon is a-*com*in' down the street. Oh, please let it be for meeeeeee!"

Olivia yawned. She liked having Flora and Ruby at the store all day, but sometimes — today, for instance — they weren't much fun. Here Olivia finally had friends with whom she could hang out, but often Flora and Ruby seemed lost in worlds of their own. It was a shame, really. Olivia, younger than her classmates but fascinated by things that held little interest for Lacey Morris or other neighborhood kids her age, had no close friends. Then along had come Ruby and Flora, and Olivia suddenly had high hopes for two built-in best friends. After all, they lived *right next door*. Olivia now spent hours, *days*, with them, but the best friendships seemed to be taking a while.

"Give it time," her mother had said. "Ruby and Flora have a lot on their minds."

Olivia closed her book and walked to the back of the store.

"You guys?" she said. "Want to take a walk or something?"

Flora turned off the sewing machine and stretched. Ruby took off the headphones.

"Okay," said Flora.

"Goody." Olivia grinned. "Going for a walk!" she called to Gigi as the girls let themselves outside. They squinted as they emerged into the sunlight. The first thing Olivia saw was Sonny Sutphin wheeling himself lazily along Main Street.

"Hi, Sonny," said Olivia.

"What's up?" asked Sonny.

"I'm reading about stalactites," said Olivia.

"My," said Sonny.

"I went to the post office twice today," said Ruby.

"And I'm sewing for Min," said Flora.

"Well, that's just fine," replied Sonny. He was peering down the street in the direction of College Pizza. "Got to go," he said suddenly. He spun his chair around and disappeared through the open door of Zack's hardware store.

Olivia and Flora and Ruby frowned at one another. Then they peered toward College Pizza.

"I wonder what . . ." Olivia's voice trailed off.

She jumped when someone touched her on the shoulder.

"My goodness! I didn't mean to startle you."

"Oh, Mr. Pennington," said Olivia. "I'm sorry. I didn't see you. I was watching Lydia. . . ." She looked at Flora and Ruby and shrugged. "Oh, well."

"Hi, Mr. Pennington," said Ruby and Flora.

"'Afternoon, ladies," replied Mr. Pennington. "Are you girls working today?"

"Sort of," said Flora.

"Do you need help with something?" asked Olivia.

"As a matter of fact, I do." Mr. Pennington reached into his pocket for a small paper bag. He opened the bag and shook out a button. "Two of these came off my good jacket," he said. "And I lost the other one, so I need to replace it. Do you have any buttons that look just like this one?"

"I think so," said Olivia. "Let's go look."

Olivia led Mr. Pennington through the store to one particular rack of buttons and turned the rack to one particular section.

"There!" she said triumphantly. "Hold your button up, Mr. Pennington. Let's compare it to some of these."

In no time, a card of buttons had been selected and Mr. Pennington was standing in line at the counter. "You certainly do know your buttons, Olivia," he said.

"Thank you," she replied. After a pause, she said, "Mr. Pennington? Do you know how to sew on buttons?"

"Well, I'm sure I do," said Mr. Pennington, but he didn't sound sure at all. "Usually, Miss Woolsey does my mending, but it seemed silly to ask her just to sew on a couple of buttons. How hard could it be?"

"It isn't hard," said Olivia. "But . . . do you have the right color thread? And scissors and a needle?"

"I think so." Mr. Pennington was scratching his head.

"Why don't I come home with you and help you?" said Olivia. She glanced at the back of the store and saw that Flora had returned to the sewing machine and Ruby was wearing the headphones again.

"Oh, there's no need for that," said Mr. Pennington.

"It's okay. I *want* to help you."

And so, several minutes later, when Min had rung up Mr. Pennington's buttons, Olivia called to her grandmother, "Gigi, I'm going to go home now." She took Mr. Pennington's arm, and they left Needle and Thread and walked down Main Street.

As Olivia turned the corner onto Aiken Avenue, she felt the small rush of contentment she always felt when she caught sight of the Row Houses, this place where she belonged no matter what, even if she had skipped a grade and even if no one else her age cared what a stalactite was or how many kinds of sparrows inhabited North America.

"Okay, if you can find a needle —" Olivia was saying a few moments later as Mr. Pennington fumbled for his key and opened the door. But she didn't finish her sentence. When she stepped inside, she was greeted by a strong odor, and the air was heavy and somehow oily.

"Mr. Pennington, I smell gas!" cried Olivia, and she felt herself begin to panic. She remembered a television show she had seen in which a gas leak had caused an entire apartment building to explode.

"The burner!" exclaimed Mr. Pennington.

He dashed into the kitchen and turned off a burner he'd left on. Olivia rushed from room to room, opening windows. The front door was wide open, and now she opened the back door, too.

"Come outside," Olivia said with a gasp. "Mr.

Pennington, come outside. Don't go back in until the smell is gone."

Olivia and Mr. Pennington sat on an iron bench in his backyard, so different from Olivia's yard next door. Hers was awash with bicycles and basketballs, an old jungle gym, and even a tent in which Olivia and her brothers sometimes liked to sleep on the hottest summer nights. Mr. Pennington's yard was tidy with rosebushes, and at the back a vegetable garden, of which Olivia was envious. Every summer, Mr. Pennington would bring bags of tomatoes and peppers and peas and beans next door to the Walters. Olivia, remembering this, realized that Mr. Pennington hadn't brought them anything yet this summer. She stood up and peered across the yard.

"Didn't you plant your vegetable garden?" she asked. She reached down to pat Jacques, who was dozing in the shade under the bench.

Mr. Pennington sighed. "No. Not this summer."

He didn't offer a reason, and Olivia didn't ask for one. Instead, she said carefully, "Mr. Pennington, did — I mean, how long do you think that burner was on?"

"Less than an hour, I'd say."

"Well, that's good, I guess," replied Olivia.

"And as you noticed, several windows were already open, since it's so hot today."

Olivia nodded. Then she stood up. "I want to go

see if the gas smell is gone," she said. She left Mr. Pennington and Jacques in the yard and returned to the house. The smell was fading, so Olivia closed the doors, but she left the windows open. She realized that her hands were shaking. It's all right, she told herself. Nothing *really* bad happened. Mr. Pennington is fine. His house is fine. Nothing blew up.

Olivia sat down hard on a kitchen chair. Nothing too bad had happened, and yet Olivia felt unsettled. She took a look around the kitchen and saw moldy fruit in a bowl on the counter. In the sink were what appeared to be several days' worth of unwashed dishes. She opened the dishwasher. Empty. She looked at the floor and saw Jacques's water dish, also empty. Olivia filled it and returned it to the floor, thinking as she did so that it was a good thing Jacques had been outside when the gas had been left on. And then it occurred to her that Jacques had been outside on his *own*. Mr. Pennington had left him to go to town. He hadn't put him on his lead in the yard. Jacques wasn't even wearing his collar. Olivia could see it hanging on the kitchen doorknob.

This wasn't good.

Olivia was trying to figure out what she should say to Mr. Pennington when he opened the back door and joined her in the kitchen.

"Olivia," he said, sounding very serious, "I need to talk to you."

"Okay." Olivia and Mr. Pennington sat down across from each other at the table.

Mr. Pennington's fingers found a saltshaker and he tapped it on the table as he spoke. "I need," he began, "I need — please don't mention this to anyone, Olivia. I'm asking you to keep this a secret. Please."

"But —"

Mr. Pennington set the shaker down and rested his hand on Olivia's arm. "Please," he said again. "No one must know about this. I'm eighty-two. If anyone finds out what happened, they'll put me in an old people's home. And I can't bear the thought of that. *This* is my home. I've lived here for more than forty years. I can't leave. Do you understand?"

Olivia thought of her own home. She had been born there. She loved her home. She loved the Row Houses. She wouldn't want to live anywhere else. And she certainly didn't want Mr. Pennington to move.

"Can we keep this a secret?" Mr. Pennington asked.

Olivia looked at his tough, wrinkled hands, at his snowy hair, into his watery brown eyes.

"Okay," she said after a moment. "It's our secret."

CHAPTER 9

The Box in the Attic

The hot weather that had arrived when June turned to July became steamier with each new day that passed. The air grew wetter, and the haze that Flora had noticed early in the month, hanging about on the horizon, whitening the edges of Camden Falls, eventually turned to clouds. The days were sultry, and Flora felt that everything she touched needed to be wrung out and tossed into a dryer. After two weeks, the overcast sky gave way to heavy dark clouds, and rain started to fall. Sometimes the sky rumbled with thunder. At night, Flora, gazing dreamily out her window, saw heat lightning in the distance.

One Sunday morning, Flora woke not only to rain but to mist. It crept past the windows on every floor of the house, as if the clouds had finally become so heavy with moisture that they dropped to the earth.

"What a gloomy day," said Min as she and Flora and Ruby sat down to their breakfast.

A crash of thunder sounded then, and Daisy Dear dove under the table and tried to bury her head between Min's knees.

"You can't hide from thunder, poor Daisy," said Min. She bent over and took Daisy's startled face between her hands.

"King doesn't mind thunder one bit," commented Ruby cheerfully as she watched King Comma wander into the kitchen and jump onto the counter.

"Now, I wonder why that is," said Min.

Ruby shook her head. "It's a mystery. A cat's mystery."

"So. What's everybody going to do today?" asked Min.

"I'm going over to the Morrises'," said Ruby. "Me and Lacey —"

"Lacey and I," Min corrected her.

"Lacey and I are going to invent a board game."

"My land, that's a wonderful idea," said Min. "What about you, Flora? Are you going to go to Olivia's?"

Flora shook her head. For reasons she didn't understand herself, she wanted to be alone on this dreary, gloomy day. And she didn't feel like answering Min's questions, but when she saw that Min was looking at her, waiting for an answer, she finally said, "I might read."

Min let her gaze linger on her granddaughter. She was used to Flora's and Ruby's moods, their quiet moments. Sometimes she asked if they wanted to talk; sometimes she said nothing. She was still deciding whether to give Flora a nudge when Ruby said, "Min, can I take tap lessons? Please? We've been here for such a long time already." (Ruby and Flora had lived in Camden Falls for one month.) "And you said I could take lessons. At home I took tap and hip-hop, and I sang in the children's chorus, and last year I got to be in two plays at the community theatre. Please can't I do something here? *Please?*"

"Yes," said Min. "You have a good point, Ruby. We will look into things. I'll ask Mrs. Morris if she knows about dance schools and so forth."

"Really? *Really*, Min?" cried Ruby, and she jumped up and threw her arms around Min, which startled Daisy Dear again, causing her to stand up and bang her head under Min's chair. In all the commotion, no one noticed Flora creep out of the kitchen and upstairs to her room.

Flora lay on her bed and listened to the sounds of the house. She heard Min singing in the kitchen. She heard Ruby slam the front door behind her as she left for Lacey's. She heard rain dripping, and a shade flapping in the breeze, and Daisy's nails clicking along the hallway. Flora stood up. She stretched. And then, without knowing why, she climbed the stairs to the third floor and pulled down the steps to the attic.

Flora had been in the attic before, helping Min store boxes under the eaves, but she had never explored it, and now that was exactly what she felt like doing. Exploring. In private. Flora pulled the string that turned on the one bulb on the attic ceiling, and then she stood in the middle of the musty room with her hands on her hips.

She recalled something Olivia had recently told her: that the attics of the Row Houses were said to be connected; that hidden in each were doors leading to the houses on either side. If a person only knew where these doors were, he could enter any house in the row without going outside. This idea both fascinated and frightened Flora. How scary it would be, she thought, to waken one night and find someone standing over your bed, someone who had crept in through your attic from another house.

Still . . . she couldn't help taking a look around for the doors. There should be one on the left (when she was facing the backyard) leading to the Malones', and one on the right leading to Olivia's. Flora pushed aside trunks and boxes and baskets and Christmas decorations. She felt along beams in the walls (pricking the palm of her hand on a splinter as she did so). She pushed at knotholes, hoping to find hidden buttons. She tried to remember all of Nancy Drew's detecting tricks. But after half an hour, she had neither seen nor felt anything resembling a door, hidden or otherwise.

Flora sat down with a little plop on the rough wooden floor. Next to her was a carton labeled SWEATERS. Beside that was one labeled MOTHER'S DISHES.

"Boring," said Flora aloud.

And then she noticed another carton, a smaller one. It appeared to be older than the others, and it wasn't labeled. Flora got to her knees. She raised the flaps of the carton. Inside was a jumble of papers and photos and albums. Some of the papers were so old they were crumbling.

Flora lifted the pile out of the box and carried it into the middle of the attic. She sat down directly under the lightbulb, the papers in her lap. On the top of the pile were three ancient postcards, all addressed to someone named Elisabeth Buestein, and all written in a foreign language that Flora guessed was German. One of the cards was dated 4.7.97, and Flora realized that 97 meant 1897.

"Wow," she said softly.

The next piece of paper was a letter written in English and dated March 22, 1927. It was from the United States Veterans Bureau in Washington and was addressed to a Mrs. Dorothy Matthews. The letter informed Mrs. Matthews that as the dependent of a deceased veteran (of World War I, Flora thought) she was entitled to a claim of $469.75, which would NOT be paid in one lump sum, but in ten (10) installments.

"That's it?" said Flora. "Her husband's dead and she gets four hundred and seventy dollars? My stars."

Flora set aside the letter and continued her search. She found a six-page typewritten document titled "A HISTORY OF RICHARD R. DAVIS, MAN OF ACTION, by his daughter, Adelaide Davis Rhinehart." On the second page was a description of the 1906 San Francisco earthquake: "About 6 AM on April 6th they were jarred by the terrible earthquake. He ran to the window to see the chimneys fall, cracks open in the streets, people running from the buildings. He called to Grace to come quickly. She ran to the window at the moment that the ceiling crashed onto their bed. It would have killed her if she hadn't jumped out in the nick of time."

"Wow," said Flora again, and she read the entire account before turning back to the box. She came to a tattered blue album with fancy gold lettering reading "My School-Days Memory Book," the first page inscribed "From Aunt Adelaide Davis to Sarah Matthews, Feb. 3, 1926." Included in the memory book, among other things, were cheers (*Hobble, gobble, razzle, dazzle, hokey, pokey, bah! A 9's, A 9's. Rah! Rah! Rah!*), autographs (*Dear Sarah, I call you "hinges" because you're something to "adore." As always, Frank*), and a list of graduation gifts received by Sarah, which included a Parker pen and pencil set, a pair of tan stockings, a pair of white stockings, a white silk slip, a bunch of sweet peas, and the memory book itself.

Flora, smiling now, continued searching through the box. Here was a War Mothers and Widows Official Certificate of Identification. Here was a marriage license, a United States Naval Reserve (Inactive) identification card, a photo of a smiling woman that had been sloppily cut from a larger photo (a pair of chubby baby hands reached out to the woman from the left edge of the picture), and here was a letter to Theodore Davis from President Harry S. Truman himself.

Flora turned back to the School-Days Memory Book. She didn't know who Sarah Matthews was, but she liked this item the best. She settled down to read it, leaning against a tattered steamer trunk, and thinking, sometimes, of her mother. She thought that her mother must have liked the attic, too. It was quiet, almost silent, although dim and a bit dusty, and she could imagine her mother sitting up here. Maybe her mother had come here when she needed to escape from her little sister, or when she was at odds with Min. Maybe she even looked through the School-Days Memory Book. Flora ran her hands over the pages, pages that her mother might once have turned. And she now understood that here in her new home, her Camden Falls roots could be revealed to her.

CHAPTER 10

The Accident

On an afternoon toward the end of July, when the sultry weather had cleared, the air was cool and clean and smelled of roses and iris, and the last of the bridal veil petals clung to the sidewalks, Min closed the door to Needle and Thread and locked it carefully. "There," she said. "Another day."

"And a good job well done," added Ruby, which was something she had heard Min say.

"Yes, a good job well done," repeated Min.

Another workweek had ended. It was Saturday, and Liz and Rick would manage the store the next afternoon. Gigi had left moments earlier. Now the locking-up had been done, and ahead of Min and Flora and Ruby stretched Saturday evening and all day Sunday.

"What shall we do tonight?" said Min.

"Could we get pizza for supper?" asked Ruby as they passed the window of College Pizza.

"I don't see why not," replied Min, and in they went to order a large pizza and a salad.

Later, they carried their supper home, Flora bearing the salad, Min carrying the pizza, and Ruby holding tight to Min's purse. They crossed Aiken Avenue, passed the first three Row Houses, and turned up their front walk.

"No one in sight," commented Flora.

"Everyone's probably out in their backyards," said Min. She was about to add that this was a perfect night for barbecuing when the toe of her shoe caught on the top step of the stoop and she stumbled and fell forward onto the granite. The pizza crashed against the front door, then dropped to the stoop, the box lid springing open.

Min let out a cry.

"Min!" exclaimed Flora, and in her surprise she dropped the salad, which spilled across the top step.

Ruby gasped. "Are you okay?" she asked her grandmother.

Min sat up. She was cradling her left wrist in her right arm. "I — I think so. No. I don't know. My wrist —"

Flora plopped onto the step next to her grandmother.

"You're sitting in lettuce!" shrieked Ruby.

"I don't care." Flora looked at Min's wrist. "Can you move it?" she asked.

Min slowly bent her wrist backward, then forward. "Yes. But it hurts."

"A lot?" asked Ruby.

"Quite a bit."

Ruby and Flora peered at Min's wrist.

"It looks all right," said Flora.

"But it feels funny," said Min. "And, oh dear, our supper is ruined."

"Don't worry," replied Ruby. "I think we have hot dogs in the fridge. We can have hot dogs tonight."

"And I can make a fresh salad," said Flora. "Come on. Let me help you up."

Flora took charge. In no time, she had settled Min in the living room and cleaned up the front stoop. Then she and Ruby made supper.

"Do you think you can eat, Min?" asked Ruby.

"Yes. If I can eat one-handed."

"You really can't use your left hand?"

Min tried switching her hot dog from her right hand to her left. She winced. "No. It hurts too much."

"I think you should go to the doctor," said Flora.

"The office is closed," replied Min. "It's Saturday night. Besides, look — my wrist isn't swollen or black and blue."

But by bedtime, her wrist *was* swollen. And she couldn't move it.

"That's it," said Flora. "We have to go to the hospital."

"How are we going to get there?" asked Ruby. "I don't think it's safe for Min to drive with just one hand."

"I'll call an ambulance."

"You will do no such thing," said Min.

"Then what should we do?" asked Flora. "You have to go, Min."

Her grandmother sighed. "All right. Call the Walters. Maybe one of them can drive me to the hospital."

Flora dialed Olivia's number. "It's their machine," she said a moment later. "Should I leave a message?"

"No," replied Min. "Hang up, honey. Let's see. Why don't you call Dr. Malone?"

Flora dialed the Malones' number. No answer. And there was no answer at the Morrises' house or the Fongs'.

Min let out another huge sigh. "All right. Try the Edwardses, and if they aren't home . . ."

"If they aren't home, I'll call Gigi," said Flora confidently.

At the Edwardses' house, Robby was sulking in front of the television. *Shrek* was playing, but Robby wasn't paying attention, and every so often he would call out, "I want to go to camp!"

Mr. Edwards was in the next room, trying to work.

Finally, he stood up, set his papers aside, crossed into the den, and sat with Robby on the couch. "I'm sorry," he said to his son. "I know you wanted to go to camp. But the camp closed."

"But *why*? I want to go swimming. I want arts and crafts —"

"I know," said his father again. "I know all these things. I understand."

Mr. Edwards tried to think about how to explain this turn of events to his son. Over the last few weeks, he and Mrs. Edwards had tried many times to make Robby understand that the camp had suddenly been discontinued, and that it had been too late in the summer to find another program for him. Robby refused to understand. He was mad, he was sad, he was frustrated, and he was at loose ends. Furthermore, his parents, both of whom had jobs, were in a bind. What were they to do for the rest of the summer? They'd been working at home more often than usual, and they had called on every sitter they could think of, but this did not solve the problem. None of the Edwardses was happy at the moment.

When the phone rang, Mr. Edwards answered it as Robby jumped up and down in front of the television, flapping his hands and shouting, "I wanted to answer it! I wanted to answer it!"

"Mr. Edwards, this is Flora Northrop," said Flora,

who then explained what had happened that evening. "So do you think you could drive us to the hospital?" she asked finally.

"Oh, boy," said Mr. Edwards, glancing at his son. "Yes, of course. But Robby will have to come with us, and he's terrified of hospitals. My wife is working late tonight. . . ." His voice trailed off. "Listen, I'll call Mrs. Edwards. Maybe she can meet us at the hospital later. I'll be in front of your house in ten minutes, okay? Don't worry, Flora. Everything will be all right."

And it was. Sort of. But not really, Flora thought later as she cast her mind over the long and troubling evening. Mr. Edwards and Robby arrived promptly, as promised, and helped Min into their car. Min sat in the front next to Mr. Edwards, and Flora and Ruby squeezed into the back with Robby. Even before they reached the hospital, Flora felt herself beginning to panic. The last time she had been on her way to a hospital was after the accident. She and Ruby had ridden in an ambulance then, but somehow this trip didn't feel much different. And Flora's mounting fear was not calmed by Robby, who kept shouting out, "Not the hospital! Not the hospital! I SAID, not the hospital!"

Mr. Edwards parked near the emergency entrance. Inside, Min explained to the nurse on duty what had happened, while Robby howled in the doorway, "I am not going in there!"

In the end, Ruby waited with Min and Mr. Edwards, while Flora sat on a bench outside the hospital with Robby. Her hands were shaking. What if, she wondered, this had been a much bigger accident? What if Min had been in a *car* accident? What if something much, much worse had happened? Much, much worse things could happen easily. They could happen quickly and they could happen when you were just riding along with your family, singing Christmas carols.

After Flora's parents had died, Min had been there to take care of Flora and Ruby. But if Min died, Flora and Ruby were out of grandparents. Flora put her head in her hands and tried to drown out the sound of Robby muttering, "Stupid hospital. Stupid, stupid hospital."

Half an hour later, with Min still waiting, Mrs. Edwards pulled into the parking lot. After a hurried conversation with her husband, she took Flora, Ruby, and Robby home. Mr. Edwards stayed behind with Min.

Flora and Ruby spent the night in the Edwardses' guest room, sleeping in oversize T-shirts loaned to them by Robby.

"Everything all right?" asked Mrs. Edwards when the girls were settled together in a double bed. She sat down in an armchair. "Do you want me to stay with you for a while?"

"That's okay," said Ruby.

"You look awfully worried. It's probably just a fracture, you know. Your grandmother might even get one of those removable casts. It isn't a big deal."

Flora forced a smile. "We're okay. Really," she said.

"All right." Mrs. Edwards tiptoed out of the room, leaving the door ajar behind her.

Ruby jumped up, closed the door, and scurried back into bed. She inched as close to her sister as she could get and tucked her feet under Flora's legs.

"Your feet are freezing!" Flora exclaimed.

"Well, the hospital was freezing."

"Put them somewhere else," said Flora.

"No. Flora? I'm scared."

Flora rolled over on her back, away from Ruby's feet, and looked at the ceiling. "Me, too," she said after a moment.

"You're not supposed to say that!" exclaimed Ruby. "You're supposed to say, 'Don't be scared, Ruby.'"

"But I am scared."

Ruby was silent. Flora could see her clasping and unclasping her hands. "What would happen to us now if something bad happened to Min?" she asked.

"Nothing bad happened to her," replied Flora.

"I know. But if something did. What would happen to us?"

Flora, who had been worrying about this very thing for hours, now felt grouchy as she heard the same questions from Ruby. She wanted to be able to tell her sister that everything would be all right. But she couldn't. "Ruby, I don't *know* what would happen, okay? I'm really sorry, but I don't know."

"Would we always be able to stay together?"

"Yes," said Flora. "I'm sure about that. You will always have me and I will always have you."

"Okay." Ruby tucked her feet back under Flora's legs, and after a while, both girls fell asleep.

When Flora and Ruby awoke the next morning, they tiptoed down to the Edwardses' kitchen in their T-shirts.

Mrs. Edwards smiled at them. "Good news," she said. "Your grandmother's at home. And she's going to be fine. Her wrist is fractured, but not badly, and she'll only need to wear a cast for a few weeks."

Ruby let out a giant sigh, as if she'd been holding her breath for the entire night, and in no time the girls had changed into their clothes, made the bed in the guest room, carefully folded Robby's T-shirts, called "Thank you!" and "Good-bye!" over their shoulders, and charged back to their house.

Min met them at the front door. "Look!" she said cheerfully. She held up her wrist, encased in its cast. "Already almost as good as new."

Ruby and Flora pounced on their grandmother, hugging her so hard she nearly lost her balance.

"Gracious me," she said. "What's all this? Come. Let's sit down — before I fall down."

Flora escorted Min into the living room, carefully guiding her by her good arm. She helped Min onto the sofa, even though Min said she could manage quite well by herself, thank you.

As soon as Flora and Ruby and Min were settled, Ruby blurted out, "Min, if anything really, really bad ever happened to you, what would happen to Flora and me?"

Flora thought Ruby could have said this a bit more tactfully, but she barely cared. She peered anxiously into Min's face.

"Oh, girls," said Min, "don't worry. You'll always be taken care of."

Flora's stomach tightened. Min hadn't said *how* they would be taken care of. And that, she felt certain, was because Min didn't know.

CHAPTER II

Sew What?

On one of the very last days of July, the cool weather still gracing Camden Falls, Nikki sat cross-legged on a patch of dry earth in front of her house. Mae sat beside her, holding out a fistful of dog kibble.

"Look, Nikki. Paw-Paw takes it right out of my hand. See?"

Sure enough, the scruffy dog nibbled delicately from Mae's outstretched palm.

"That's great, Mae," said Nikki absently. Her mind was on the arrival of Mrs. DuVane, and her ears were pricked for the sound of tires on gravel.

"Nikki?" said Mae a few moments later.

"What?"

"I *said*, isn't it too bad we have to keep Paw-Paw a secret?" She paused. "Aren't you listening?"

"I'm sorry," said Nikki. "I guess I'm just thinking about the old — I mean, about Mrs. DuVane. That's all."

"She's coming today, right?"

"Any minute now."

"And where's she taking you?"

"Into town to that sewing store. For some kind of lesson."

"I want to learn to sew," said Mae.

"Every time I get back from the store I'll teach you what I learned, okay?"

"Okay. . . . Nikki? Who's going to watch me while you're in town?"

"Mom's here."

Mae lowered her voice. "She's *asleep*."

"Oh. Already?" Mrs. Sherman was having another bad day. "Well, you know the rules. If Tobias and I aren't here, you have to stay on our property. So just . . . keep quiet so you don't disturb Mom, and stay out of Dad's way if he comes home. Maybe Tobias will be back soon."

At that moment, Nikki heard gravel crunching. Mrs. DuVane honked twice and waved gaily out her car window. "Hello, Nikki dear! Ready for your big day?"

Nikki rolled her eyes, then kissed the top of Mae's head before starting toward the car. "Hi, Mrs. DuVane," she said flatly as she opened the door.

Mrs. DuVane eyed Nikki's dusty shorts and her

smudged legs. "Is that how you're going to go to the store?" she asked. Without waiting for an answer, she glanced at her watch, then said, "Well, you haven't time to change. But next week, Nicolette, try to look a bit more presentable."

"Okay," said Nikki. "I mean, yes, ma'am."

Nikki stared out the window as Mrs. DuVane drove into Camden Falls. She didn't feel like speaking.

Mrs. DuVane parked her car across from Needle and Thread. "Now remember, Nicolette," she said as they climbed out of the Audi and closed the doors behind them, "this embroidery class is for adults, so you won't be able to participate per se, but there are usually two or three other little girls here at the store, so maybe they can teach you some things while I'm taking the class. You can all learn from one another!" She added brightly, "Sewing is a very respectable pastime."

"Yes, ma'am," mumbled Nikki.

When Mrs. DuVane opened the door to Needle and Thread, a bell rang. Nikki stepped into the cool air of the store and was engulfed by the smell of new fabric, of coffee, and of something sweet she thought might be cookies.

"Hello, Mrs. DuVane," called a woman from behind the counter. "You're just in time for the class."

Mrs. DuVane smiled. "And I've brought someone with me," she said. "This is Nicolette. I know she can't take the class, but I thought she might enjoy looking around the store. Nicolette is very creative. Aren't you, dear?"

"I like to draw," said Nikki, staring down at a piece of tape that was stuck to the floor.

"Hey!" called a voice, and Nikki turned around. Sitting on some couches at the front of the store were three girls about her age, and spread on a table in front of them were squares of fabric, which the girls were cutting into shapes and arranging in patterns. "You're Nikki Sherman, aren't you?" said one of the girls.

"Yeah," said Nikki. She couldn't believe her bad luck. This girl — Olivia Walton? Was that her name? — had actually said to her on the school playground just a couple of months ago, "You know, if you washed your clothes more often, they'd smell better."

Nikki had stared at her. This tiny little girl (she was in Nikki's grade, but not in her class, and Nikki thought she might have skipped a grade at some point), this tiny little girl had had the *nerve* to tell Nikki how to do her housework. Let *her* try to wash clothes in a machine that didn't work half the time. This girl probably didn't even have to *do* her family's laundry.

When Nikki hadn't been able to stop staring, Olivia finally said, "I — I didn't mean anything by that. I hope I didn't hurt your feelings. I just thought you'd like to know that there's an easy way . . ." Her voice began to trail off. ". . . an easy way to, um, to improve your personal hygiene."

At this point, Nikki, disgusted, shook her head, turned around, and walked off. Her only wish then had been that she not wind up in Olivia's class in the fall.

And now here she was, facing Olivia and two of her friends. Worse, she was stuck with them for an entire hour.

"Come on and sit with us," said Olivia. "Our grand-mothers gave us a job. There's a kids' patchwork pillow class coming up, and we're supposed to make up designs for some easy pillows. You can help us."

Nikki sniffed pointedly at her underarms. "If you're sure I won't oh-fend you," she said, and was pleased to note that Olivia's cheeks reddened slightly.

Three couches were arranged around the table. Olivia and one of the girls sat on one, and the third girl, the youngest-looking one, sat on another. Nikki sat down by herself in the middle of the remaining couch. She eyed Olivia's friends.

"Um," said Olivia, "do you want to help us? Our grandmothers —"

"Am I supposed to know who your grandmothers are?" asked Nikki.

"They own this store," spoke up the girl who was sitting next to Olivia.

"Wow," said Nikki. "The *owners*."

After a brief pause, the girl spoke again. "Do you know how to sew?"

Nikki hesitated. She frequently mended the clothes

that got tossed into a wicker basket sitting in the corner of the kitchen, but she had a feeling this wasn't the kind of sewing the girl meant.

"I can sew a little," she said at last.

"Have you done any quilting?" asked Olivia.

"No."

"Well, that's okay."

"I know it's okay."

"Hey!" exclaimed Olivia after a few moments, during which Nikki had sat glaring at the fabric pieces and no one had spoken. "I just realized we haven't introduced ourselves. Well, you know me. I'm Olivia Walter." (Oh, *Walter*, thought Nikki.) "But you don't know Flora and Ruby. This is Flora, and this is Ruby," she said, pointing to each of them. "Flora and Ruby Northrop. And this" (she pointed to Nikki) "is Nikki Sherman. She's in my grade. Flora and Ruby just moved to Camden Falls. Flora is going to be in our grade, too, Nikki. Ruby will be in fourth."

Nikki, looking desperately at the pieces of fabric being arranged on the table and having no idea what to do with them, finally said, "So how come you guys moved here? Did your father get a new job or something?"

At this, silence fell. Flora went still as stone, then began arranging the fabric again, her eyes boring into the table. Ruby slid back onto the couch for a moment, then moved forward and whisked a triangle of blue calico away from Flora. Wordlessly, Flora grabbed it back from her.

"That's mine!" cried Ruby.

"No, it isn't. I was using it."

"But I had it before and I need it to go right here. See? I'm making a *star*? SEE?"

"Then cut your own triangle. That's why we have scissors. Anyway, a star pattern is going to be too complicated for beginners."

"I'm a beginner, and I'm making a star."

"Well, stop."

From across the couch, Olivia eyed Nikki. "Nice move," she said.

"What? What did I do?"

"Flora and Ruby moved here because their parents . . . their parents . . ."

"Go ahead and say it. Our parents died." Ruby grabbed a pair of scissors and cut a sloppy triangle out of the calico fabric. "We're orphans," she added, slamming the triangle down on the table.

"I'm sorry," said Nikki, and now she could feel her own face flushing. "I'm *really* sorry."

"It's all right," said Flora.

"You didn't know," added Olivia. "Okay, come on. Here. Cut all these pieces of fabric into four-inch squares."

Nikki took the fabric and scissors that Olivia held toward her, but she said, "Are you always so bossy?"

"Pretty much." Olivia turned back to Flora and Ruby. "Now, I think that all the pillows should be made up of squares only. That's easier for beginners. Nine squares will make up into a very nice pillow."

Flora let out a sigh. "Okay. Half the fun is in choosing the fabric anyway, seeing which ones look best together. Ruby, quit working on that star. Put the triangle pieces away."

"No!" Ruby slid away from the older girls, and for a while, Nikki, Olivia, and Flora concentrated on laying out squares.

"With squares you could make theme pillows," commented Flora. "You could use this fabric with the Eiffel Tower on it, and this one with the globes, and this one with the French poodles to make a Paris pillow."

"You could do the same thing with stars," muttered Ruby, coming back to the group. And after a moment, she added, "I'd *much* rather be in a tap class right now."

Nikki glanced at her, then back at the table, where she halfheartedly began arranging squares of fabric again.

"What's your theme?" Olivia asked Ruby a few moments later.

"I don't *know*, okay? I'm just experimenting."

"Hey," said Nikki, "didn't you say you were supposed to come up with several patterns for the class? Now you only have the pillows made from nine squares."

"And the stars!" cried Ruby.

"Would you forget about the stars?" shouted Olivia.

"Girls, what's going on over there?" called Min.

"Nothing."

Half an hour later, when Mrs. DuVane's embroidery class ended, Nikki, Ruby, Flora, and Olivia were still sitting on the couches, but they were sitting as far from one another as they could manage.

"This store," said Nikki, getting to her feet, "should be called Sew What?"

"Ha-ha," said Olivia as Mrs. DuVane appeared, smiling and clutching a square of muslin adorned with ribbon flowers and bees.

"Well, that was a wonderful class, just wonderful," said Mrs. DuVane. "I hope you girls had fun. Nicolette, let's buy you a few supplies and then we should be on our way." She turned to Flora, Ruby, and Olivia. "We'll be back again next week."

"Goody," muttered Olivia.

CHAPTER 12

Olivia's Secret

Olivia, leaning against the counter in Needle and Thread, wrapped her fingers around the bills in her pocket. One five and two ones. Olivia felt like spending them. And she felt like doing it alone. The previous afternoon was still fresh in her mind, and desperate as she was for friends, she found herself tired of Ruby's whining and Flora's moods. The three of them had spent a tense morning together at Needle and Thread, nobody wanting to admit that they had actually had a fight. But now Olivia was ready for an escape. Also, she was fearful that Ruby or Flora would ask her what Nikki had meant by "If you're sure I won't oh-fend you," and she did *not* feel like having to explain it.

After a morning spent affixing price tags to the fabric remnants that were being added to the sales bin, Olivia wanted to wander around downtown before returning to Aiken Avenue, so she called to Gigi, "I'm going now!" and headed out into the heat that had returned to Camden Falls.

She nearly collided with Scary Mary Woolsey, who was on her way in.

"Sorry! I'm sorry!" said Olivia quickly, and she held the door open for Mary, who ducked her head and hustled inside the store.

Olivia closed the door and let her breath out in a rush. She stood in front of the bench and glanced up and down Main Street. Her fingers closed over the seven dollars again. Seven whole dollars. What did she feel like doing with her money? There were many possibilities.

Town was quiet. Olivia was thinking about going to Camden Falls Art Supply for butterfly stickers when she heard shouting and laughing. She glanced down the street and saw a group of older kids, boys and girls. They were sauntering along Main Street in a pack, whooping and high-fiving one another.

Olivia plopped down on the bench. She eyed the kids.

"Give it," said one, snatching a baseball cap away from another.

"Ooh, tough guy," said one of the girls.

"Let's get something to eat."

"Samuels won't let us in his store anymore."

"Forget him. We'll go get pizza."

The kids were all talking at once, and Olivia felt threatened by them, even though they hadn't noticed her.

"We can swipe something from the grocery store," one was saying. "Samuels won't notice us."

"Why don't you stop talking about it and actually do it?" said a voice, and the voice was familiar. Olivia realized it belonged to Lydia Malone. Sure enough, there she was in the middle of the group of kids.

"Look," said a girl whose name, Olivia thought, was Brandi. Brandi grabbed Lydia by the wrist and pointed to a sign advertising the 350th birthday celebration for Camden Falls. "Oh, cool. Whoa. Three hundred and fifty *years*. Let's celebrate! Par-*tay*!"

"Don't you want to enter the photography show? Or how about the art show?" said the boy who had grabbed the baseball hat. "Mommy, Mommy, look at my painting! . . . Hey, we could have our own float in the parade. We could dress up as Pilgrims!" The boy ripped the sign off a lamppost and threw it in a trash can.

Brandi now pointed down the street. "Look, it's the retard, you guys," she said. She let her tongue protrude from her mouth and she loped around the sidewalk in a circle. "Duh, one plus one makes, duh, I don't know."

Olivia rose to her feet. She could feel her face burning. If that girl was talking about Robby . . .

And at that moment, Olivia was greeted by a shout. "Olivia! Olivia! Hello, Olivia!"

Robby, accompanied by a sitter, was hurrying along Main Street. He skirted the crowd of older kids in his rush to reach Olivia.

"Hi, Robby," said Olivia. She turned to glare at Lydia. Lydia lowered her eyes, but Brandi danced up and down behind Robby, like Squirrel Nutkin in one of Olivia's picture books. And she inscribed circles in the air with her index finger, pointing at his head. Crazy.

Well, thought Olivia. It just goes to show. Brandi doesn't know a thing about Down syndrome. Robby isn't crazy.

"We're on our way to Zack's!" exclaimed Robby. "We need sandpaper, Olivia."

"Have fun," Olivia called as Robby and his sitter turned toward the hardware store.

Olivia, feeling braver, glared at Lydia and her friends, but they had passed her by now, too, preparing to cross Main Street. Olivia could hear Brandi say, "There must be a way to sneak into the movie theatre without paying."

"Isn't that cheating?" asked one of the boys.

"No, dolt," said Lydia. "Cheating is like when you look at someone else's paper when you're taking a test."

"But we're cheating the theatre out of money."

"So go home," replied Lydia. And the kid broke away from the group and walked angrily down the sidewalk.

Olivia didn't feel like shopping anymore. She walked along Main Street and turned toward Aiken Avenue and the Row Houses. When she reached her own house, she hesitated, then crossed the lawn to Mr. Pennington's stoop.

"Olivia!" exclaimed Mr. Pennington when he answered his door. "How nice to see you. How are you doing?"

"I'm fine," said Olivia, doing her best to put Lydia and her friends out of her mind.

"Really? You don't quite seem fine."

Olivia sighed. She followed Mr. Pennington into his kitchen, checking along the way to make sure things were as they should be. The hallway was tidy. That was a good sign. And Jacques's water bowl was full. The sink didn't look too bad, either, but Olivia decided she'd clean it up before she went home.

Olivia sank into a chair in the kitchen. "Some kids were teasing Robby in town," she said. "I don't think he noticed, but . . ." Olivia paused. "That just makes me so mad."

"Lots of things are unfair," said Mr. Pennington, sitting down across the table from Olivia. "You should have heard what kids called me when I was going to school."

Olivia could imagine. "No one's ever called me anything too bad," she said, "but once in third grade this girl said I looked like I had stuck my finger in a socket. You know, because of my hair."

"That isn't even very original," said Mr. Pennington, and Olivia smiled.

It was later, when Olivia was tidying up Mr. Pennington's kitchen, that he disappeared for a few minutes, then returned with a small box. "Olivia," he said, "I'd like for you to have this."

Olivia turned around. She dried her hands, then picked up the box, which was made from dark wood, with a carving of an iris on the top. "It's beautiful," she said.

"It belonged to my wife. Before that, it belonged to her mother. I think you should have it. Let me tell you how Mrs. Pennington used it. At night, she would tell her worries to it before she went to bed. She banished them to the box, and she said that in the morning, they were always gone."

"A worry box!" said Olivia. "Thank you!" She threw her arms around Mr. Pennington's waist and hugged him.

Later, as she walked back to her house, Olivia's fingers closed over the box in her pocket. She was still fingering it when she noticed her father's car in the street. Hmm. Too early for that. Why was he home from work so soon?

Olivia stepped through the door of her house and found her parents standing together in the front hall.

"What's wrong?" Olivia asked. "I know something's wrong."

Her parents turned to face her. "Olivia," said her father, "I lost my job today."

CHAPTER 13

Stitches

Main Street, Flora had often heard Min say, was unpredictable. You could never tell when it was going to be quiet and when it was going to be busy. If a rainy day was quiet, someone was bound to say, "It's the weather. Everyone just wants to hole up at home." If a rainy day was busy, someone else would say, "It's the weather. Everyone's bored so they've all come into town to shop." If a weekend day was busy, especially during the summer, someone would say, "It's all the tourists." If a weekend day was quiet, someone else would say, "There's just no telling. Everyone has so much to do these days. Nobody has time for shopping."

It was on an unaccountably quiet Saturday, a glorious summer morning with insect wings whispering through the soft air and birds calling from the ash trees, that Min and Gigi looked at each other in their deserted store and shook their heads. "I thought this would be one of the busiest weekends of the summer," said Min. "Except for the holiday weekends."

"So did I," said Gigi.

"Well, I'm glad it's quiet," said Flora. "I feel like sewing. There won't be any classes here today, will there?"

"No," said Min. "So I suppose this will be a good time to take care of all those things we never seem to get around to."

"Do you have any sewing for me to do?" asked Flora.

"As a matter of fact, yes," replied Min. "And Ruby, you can help Flora, if you'd like."

"What do you want us to do?" asked Ruby.

"Look around the store," said Min. "See all the sample projects we've displayed?" She indicated a crib quilt hanging from the ceiling, a mannequin modeling a woman's lacy blouse, another modeling a boy's summer suit, and here and there smaller projects: a quilted eyeglass case, an embroidered pillow, a set of linen placemats. "Guess where they came from," said Min.

"You and Gigi made them?" guessed Flora.

Min nodded. "Mary, too. Now it's time to change the displays, though. They've been up for a while. We need autumn ones. We'll put out the vest and skirt you made, Flora, but we need a few other things. Would you two like to work on some?"

"Can we make anything we like?" asked Flora.

"Pretty much."

"Could I choose a pattern and make a jumper?"

"Absolutely. That's a great idea."

"I'm not good enough to make any of those things by myself," said Ruby. "I'd need help."

"I have an idea," said Gigi. "How would you like to make new signs to place around the store? We need some cards to describe the displays and to advertise specials and new items that have come in. If I told you what to write on the cards, would you make them? You could decorate them with markers and buttons and rickrack, anything you like."

"Yes!" said Ruby. "Cool! Signs for the store."

So Min and Gigi gave Ruby some paper and other materials and set her up at a table.

Flora, meanwhile, feeling the surge of happiness that accompanied any new project, sat down with a stack of pattern books and began to page through them. As far as she was concerned, this was the best part of any project — planning it: figuring out what she wanted to do, gathering her materials and supplies, and looking ahead to the fun she would have and the sense of satisfaction she would feel when the project had been completed.

"Why don't you make the jumper in your size," said Min, "so you can wear it when we take it down next month."

"Really?" said Flora. "Thank you. That would be

great. Oh, Min, I just thought of something. I'm going to need to wash the fabric before I cut out the pieces."

"You can run it over to the Laundromat behind the grocery store," said Min. "That will be the fastest way."

Flora returned to the pattern books. Fifteen minutes later, she had narrowed her choices to two jumpers, and when she went looking through the pattern drawers and found that one wasn't available in her size, her decision was made.

"Look, Min," she said. "I'm going to make this one. Do you think I can do it?" Flora held out the pattern. It was for a loose jumper with a low neckline and a slightly raised bodice.

"I do think so. This is a good decision, Flora. You don't need to put in a zipper, since you can unbutton the shoulder straps. You've made straps before, haven't you?"

"Yes."

"And buttonholes?"

"Yes. With the machine."

"You'll need to line the bodice. Do you think you can do that?"

"I might need a little help," confessed Flora. "And also, I want to pipe the edges of the straps. I've seen that in pictures, but I haven't done it before."

Now came another of Flora's favorite tasks. Pattern in hand, she wandered through the racks of fabric and tried to envision her jumper. Of course, she could make it look just like the one on the cover of the pattern, but she wanted to be original. Flora was poring over the selection of quilting cottons, in all sorts of colors and prints, when she was startled to discover that she could hear her mother's voice in her head. "It's all about the fabric," her mother reminded her, something she had said many times. Mrs. Northrop hadn't taken as great an interest in sewing as Min or Flora did, but every now and then, Flora remembered, her mother would suddenly be struck with an idea for something she wanted to make and would rush off to the fabric store and return with everything she needed for her latest creation.

"All about the fabric," Flora repeated. In a way, her mother was right. With the simple pattern Flora had chosen, she could make a fancy jumper out of velveteen, or a more traditional one out of corduroy, or a fun one by piecing together coordinating cotton prints.

Flora pretended she was with her mother, that they were walking arm in arm through Needle and Thread, and in this way, she decided on the fun version of the dress, which she knew would have pleased her mother. She chose coordinating ginghams and florals and was starting to think about making the front of the skirt out of one print and the back out of another, but suddenly she heard her mother's voice again, this time saying, "Less is more. Don't go overboard."

"I've made my choices," Flora announced to Min,

approaching the cutting table with the bolts of fabric, and she explained what she planned to do. "How am I ever going to wait for all this to get washed?" said Flora. "I want to start working on it right now."

Min and Gigi sent Flora and Ruby on errands while the fabric spun around in the machine at the Soap Box.

"Ruby," said Flora as they sat in College Pizza, waiting for their lunch order, "do you ever pretend you can talk to Mom and Dad?"

She half expected a smart answer from her sister, but Ruby looked seriously at Flora and replied, "I don't exactly pretend I can talk to them, but sometimes I feel like they're with me, like they can see what I'm doing. Not like they're in heaven looking down at me, but like they're really right next to me. Somehow."

Flora nodded. "I felt Mom with me at the store this morning, helping me with my project. At first it was weird, but after a while it felt sort of comforting. Plus, she was giving me good advice."

Ruby smiled. "I'm going to pretend Mom and Dad are with me this afternoon while I finish making the signs. Mom will tell me to check my spelling and Dad will say, 'Are you *sure* that's what you want to do?' when I'm about to make a mistake."

"This morning I could hear Mom say, 'Less is more,'" said Flora. "Remember how she would always say that? Instead of saying something was tacky?"

"And sometimes she would say, 'My stars,' just like Min."

After lunch, Flora collected her washed fabric from the Soap Box. For the next few hours, as she laid out her pattern and pinned and cut out the pieces and began stitching her dress, she felt her mother by her side, heard her reminders, her encouragement, too, and the day passed more quickly and pleasantly than any had in a long time.

CHAPTER 14

Pocket Money

The dry spell ended and the customers returned to Main Street. Needle and Thread grew busy again.

"Min, I can't find the patterns for the embroidery class," said Flora one morning.

"Min, what should I do with the new magazines?" asked Ruby.

"Hey, is that Nikki girl going to be here again today?" Flora abandoned her search for the patterns and approached Olivia, who was waiting on a customer.

"Just a sec," said Olivia. "Let me finish this first."

Olivia had begun working at Needle and Thread. After her father's announcement, she had decided to get a job; she should be earning her own pocket money. She told her parents they didn't need to give her an allowance anymore, and now she worked at the store. She was to work for just a couple of hours each day — Gigi wouldn't let her work more than that — but this would more than make up for the allowance she'd been receiving.

Flora and Ruby, while sad to hear about Mr. Walter's job, were pleased to be able to spend more time with their new friend (their argument was forgotten), although Olivia was very serious about her work and didn't talk much to Flora and Ruby when she was busy.

Olivia now handed the customer his change and turned to Flora. "What did you say?" she asked.

"I was wondering if Nikki will be here again. Today's the day of the second ribbon embroidery class. When that lady Mrs. DuVane came the first time, she brought Nikki with her."

"We'll find out pretty soon if she's going to be here," said Ruby, looking at her watch. "The class starts in half an hour."

"Nikki has a bad attitude," muttered Olivia. But as she was saying this, she recalled her words about Nikki's personal hygiene and wished she could take them back. She had the uncomfortable suspicion that perhaps she was the cause of Nikki's bad attitude — even though she had just been trying to help.

Olivia stepped away from the cash register. Her customer had left, and now the store was quiet.

"Flora, did you find the patterns?" asked Min. She climbed on a stool to check a shelf over Mary's work space.

"Min! Get down," yelped Flora. "I'll look there."

Min stepped down and reached behind the counter for a knitting needle. She inserted it in her cast and wiggled it around. "My land, this cast makes me itchy," she said. "I can't wait to get it off."

"How many more weeks?" asked Olivia.

"Just a couple," replied Min.

"Oh, but you'll still have it on for the party. That's too bad."

"What party?" asked Ruby.

"The Row House party. I mentioned it, I think," said Min.

"Did you?" said Ruby. "I don't remember."

"Me, neither," said Flora.

"Row House parties are always fun," said Olivia. "I'll tell you about them during the class. I have to work until then."

"No, you don't," said Gigi. "You're done. You started early today." Gigi opened the cash register and pulled out a few bills. "Here you go, sweetie. Here's your pay. Good job. Thank you so much."

Olivia hugged her grandmother. "Come on, you guys," she said to Flora and Ruby, and she pulled them to one of the couches.

"Olivia," said Ruby slowly as the girls sat down. "About your father's job . . ."

Olivia said nothing.

"Well, I think it's very unfair that he got fi — I mean that he got . . ."

"Downsized," supplied Flora uncomfortably.

"I have a feeling he knew it was going to happen," said Olivia. "He hadn't been happy at work for a long time. He says that now he can decide what he really, really wants to do."

"But who's earning the money —" Ruby was asking when Flora nudged her in the side with her elbow.

"Ow!" said Ruby.

"It's okay," said Olivia. "Mom and Dad said we'll be all right for a while. And I guess Gigi and Poppy could help us out. . . ." Her voice trailed off. Then she brightened. "Let me tell you about the party," she said. "We have parties at the Row Houses pretty often. Everyone who lives there comes. Sometimes we have them for special occasions, like birthdays and holidays, but sometimes we have them just because we want to. This one is going to be a barbecue, and we're going to have it in the backyards. Everyone will bring something. There'll be hot dogs and hamburgers and potato salad and fruit salad and dessert and ice cream. It'll be great."

"I'm going to make two lemon meringue pies," called Min from the cutting counter.

"Oh, yum," said Olivia. "And my mom is going to make deviled eggs and my dad is going to grill corn on the cob. Hey, you know what, you guys?" Olivia turned to Ruby and Flora. "I think we should be in charge of games for all the kids."

"That's a wonderful idea," said Min.

"Hey, there she is," said Ruby suddenly in a loud whisper. At that moment, the door to Needle and Thread opened and in walked Mrs. DuVane, followed by Nikki.

"Why, look, Nicolette," said Mrs. DuVane. "Here are your friends. Right where we left them last week."

Olivia looked at Nikki, whose face did not display the expression of a person greeting old friends. In fact, she looked, Olivia thought, like a caged bird just waiting for her owner to mistakenly leave the door open so she could escape.

But Mrs. DuVane was here for the class, which meant Nikki was stuck in Needle and Thread for another hour. Which meant that Olivia, Ruby, and Flora were stuck with Nikki.

When none of the girls spoke, Mrs. DuVane hesitated, then said, "Well, you have fun now!"

"We didn't have fun the first time," muttered Nikki.

"What was that?" asked Mrs. DuVane.

"She *said*," spoke up Olivia loudly, "that we di —"

"Good afternoon, Mrs. DuVane," said Gigi then.

"Come join us. Were you able to practice at home this week?"

Gigi whisked Mrs. DuVane toward the back of the store.

In the front, Nikki glowered at Ruby, Olivia, and Flora. Ruby, Olivia, and Flora looked at one another.

"You know, I was thinking," said Flora finally. "About last week. I was thinking — now don't take this the wrong way —"

Uh-oh, thought Ruby.

"— that maybe you know how to sew a little bit, but you only know the basics, like how to sew a straight seam or something. Maybe you haven't made pillows or quilts or —"

"Flora's really good at sewing," interrupted Olivia loyally.

"Whoopee," said Nikki.

"Look. Seriously," said Flora. "I can show you how to make a patchwork pillow. It's easy."

"Look. Seriously," said Nikki. "I don't care."

But Flora was already off in search of supplies. She rummaged through the scrap bin by Mary Woolsey's work space and returned to the front of the store with a handful of calico squares. She dropped them on the coffee table and left again. When she returned the second time, she was carrying a pair of scissors, a plastic square, a package of needles, and a spool of thread. "Here," said Flora. "This is all you need to make a patchwork pillow. And you can have all these things. For free. Except the scissors. Those belong to my grandmother."

Nikki, who had sat down on one of the couches, now stood up. "I am not," she said fiercely, "a charity case."

"I didn't mean —" Flora started to say.

But Olivia had jumped to her feet, too. "She's just being nice to you, Nikki."

"I don't need anyone to be nice to me. I don't even want to be here."

"Well, don't take it out on us," said Flora.

"Yeah, we didn't ask you to come," added Ruby. "And anyway, some of us wish we weren't here, either. I'd rather be in a dance class."

"Are you *still* talking about that?" exclaimed Nikki. "That's what you were babbling about last week. If you want to take a class so badly, then go find one instead of sitting here complaining all day."

Ruby didn't say anything. Instead, she crossed her arms and turned around on the couch, her back to Nikki. So Nikki crossed her arms and turned her back, and then Olivia and Flora did the same, even though they were only mad at Nikki, not at each other — although Olivia finally had to admit that she was also mad at herself, which made her feel very crabby indeed.

CHAPTER 15

Stuff 'n' Nonsense

Ruby stood at the front door of Needle and Thread and looked outside at the wet street. Rain had fallen all morning. The store, brighter than usual on this dark day, smelled of wet pavement and also of wet dog, since Mr. Pennington had stopped by the store with Jacques and was now sitting on the couch having a cup of coffee with Min, during a quiet moment before the ribbon embroidery class began. Directly across the street was Stuff 'n' Nonsense. Even from where she stood, Ruby could see the rows and rows of china animals in the window. Next to Stuff 'n' Nonsense was the T-shirt Emporium, and next to that the Gourmet Shop. Ruby watched people enter and leave the stores. She felt around in her pockets. No money to spend. She turned and flopped on the couch next to Mr. Pennington and Jacques and scratched Jacques's ears.

"Bored, sweetie?" Min asked Ruby.

"A little."

"I have a job for you. Would you like a job?"

"Okay."

"Mrs. Edwards ordered some special fabric a couple of weeks ago. It just came in. Would you like to take it to her house?"

"Definitely." Ruby glanced at Flora and Olivia, who were designing a large fabric butterfly for Olivia's bedroom. They'd been working for an hour. Ruby knew she was welcome to join them, but she wasn't interested in large fabric butterflies. And at the moment, Olivia and Flora seemed interested in nothing else.

Min excused herself, left Mr. Pennington and Jacques, and pulled an N&T shopping bag from behind the checkout counter.

"Here you go, Ruby," she said. "Mrs. Edwards has already paid for this, so all you have to do is deliver it."

"What if no one's home?" asked Ruby.

"Don't worry," said Mr. Pennington. "Robby's there. Margaret is sitting for him."

"Okay." Ruby skipped out of the store, her mood improved. She liked both Margaret and Robby. Margaret, she thought, was nothing like Lydia. She was sweet and patient, thought up good games to play, and liked to hug. And Robby — well, Robby was the most enthusiastic person Ruby had ever met.

When Ruby rang the bell at the Edwardses' house, she was greeted by a shout from inside. "I'LL GET IT!" cried Robby's voice.

"Remember to find out who's there *before* you open the door," Ruby could hear Margaret say.

There was a thump from in the hallway, and then Robby called out, "Tell me who's there because I can't let a stranger in!"

"Robby, it's me, Ruby Northrop. I have a package from the store for your mom."

"Margaret, it's Ruby, who is not a stranger!"

"Okay. Open the door."

The door was flung open and Robby cried, "Hi, Ruby! It stopped raining, but Margaret Malone and I are playing Go Fish anyway."

"As soon as we finish this game, though," said Margaret, joining Robby in the hallway, "we're going outside. We thought we'd take a walk into town," she added, turning to Ruby.

Ruby held out the bag. "This is for Mrs. Edwards," she said. "It's some fabric she ordered. Min said it's already paid for."

"Thank you, Ruby," said Robby solemnly. "I will put it right here in the kitchen — Hey! This is the material for my pajamas. Mom is going to make me Batman pajamas! Oh, boy! Batman pajamas! Okay, let's go into town!" Robby jumped up and down, hands flapping.

"Robby, don't you want to finish our game?" asked Margaret.

"No, I'm too excited! Let's go now. Right now. Oh, boy! Batman pajamas!"

So Ruby walked back to Main Street with Robby and Margaret.

Robby was quiet as they passed the Row Houses, then said suddenly, "Ruby, do you like living here? Mom and Dad said it might take a while. But do you like it? Do you like Camden Falls? I like living here."

Ruby smiled. "I guess I'm still getting used to it. But I like it."

"Good," said Robby. He paused. "Do you miss your mom and dad?"

"Robby," said Margaret, and she put her arm around his shoulder, "remember when we talked about sensitive subjects? This would be a sensitive subject. And it might be better for you to wait and see if Ruby brings it up herself."

Robby hung his head. "Okay," he mumbled.

Ruby looked from Robby to Margaret. "It's all right," she said. "I do miss my mom and dad, but every day it gets just a teensy bit better."

"That's what I found out after my mother died," spoke up Margaret.

Ruby looked at her with interest. She knew that Margaret and Lydia's mother had died — she didn't remember a visit to the Row Houses when there had been a Mrs. Malone — but she didn't know what had happened or when. She was just wondering if this might be some sort of secret, when Robby said, "Margaret, can you tell Ruby what happened to your mother?" He paused, then gave Margaret a sly smile. "You brought up the sensitive subject yourself."

Margaret smiled back at him. "Yes, I did. Ruby, my mother died five and a half years ago."

Ruby did some mental arithmetic. Margaret and Lydia must have lost their mother when they were about the same ages as Ruby and Flora were now.

"She had something called a brain aneurysm," Margaret was saying. "She died very suddenly."

"I'm sorry," said Ruby as they turned the corner onto Main Street. "Margaret, can I ask you something? If it's too sensitive, you don't have to answer."

"You can ask me anything," said Margaret.

"Do you still remember what your mother looked like?"

Margaret's smile faded slightly, and when she began speaking again, her voice was softer. "Yes. But I can't see her in my mind as easily as I could at first. That's why I keep lots of photos of her in my room."

Ruby was going to ask Margaret another question, but then she heard Robby say, "Two whole dollars." He thrust his hand into his pocket and pulled out two one-dollar bills. "Ruby, I have two dollars to spend today! Dad gave me money this morning. I want to spend it right here. In Stuff 'n' Nonsense. I can get *lots* of things for two dollars. Someday I'm going to *work* in Stuff 'n' Nonsense. That would be a very good job."

"All right then," said Margaret as they stood outside the store. "In we go. Would you like to come with us, Ruby?"

Ruby nodded and followed Robby and Margaret through the door.

"Wow," said Robby. "Oh boy, oh boy, oh boy." He waved his hands in front of his face as he looked around the store.

"Robby, settle down," said Margaret quietly, glancing at Mrs. Grindle, who was standing by the checkout counter, her hand on her hip.

"Remember that many of the items in the store are fragile," Mrs. Grindle said, her lips pursed.

Ruby had been about to pick up a china dolphin that she thought would look nice in her collection (I could name her Delphine, she thought), but now she withdrew her hand.

Mrs. Grindle stood before her new customers, eyeing them suspiciously. Ruby eyed her back. Mrs. Grindle was tall and skinny as a rake, her hair pulled severely back from her face, spectacles perched on her pointy nose. She looked, Ruby realized, like the illustration of the witch from *Hansel and Gretel* in an old storybook of Ruby and Flora's. Ruby wondered why Mrs. Grindle, who apparently didn't like children any more than the witch did, owned a store that sold so many toys.

Robby, calmer now, made his way to a wall of stickers and surveyed them, his hands clasped behind his back. "Do you know why stickers are good, Ruby?" he asked. "Because you can get so many and still have money left over to spend on" (he glanced at Mrs. Grindle) "other *fragile items*."

Robby walked around and around the store, studying small objects and their price tags, muttering to himself, adding figures in his head, and sometimes counting on his fingers.

"The challenge for Robby," Margaret told Ruby, "is to see how *many* things he can get for his money. This could take a while."

Ruby followed Robby for a few moments, then lost interest, especially since she didn't have any of her own money to spend. She thought about returning to Needle and Thread but remembered that the embroidery class would be in progress, which meant that Nikki Sherman would be across the street, and Ruby didn't feel like spending another hour in Nikki's unpleasant company.

Ruby watched Mrs. Grindle scowl as she unpacked a carton of newly arrived toys. She examined a display of necklaces by the door. Then she started down an aisle crammed with candles and ornaments and little ruffled pillows but stopped when she noticed someone standing at the other end of the aisle. Nikki Sherman. She was looking intently at a row of dog figurines.

Nikki? What was she doing here? She was supposed to be at Needle and Thread. Maybe, thought Ruby, Nikki didn't want to hang around with Ruby and Flora and Olivia any more than they wanted to hang around with her. Ruby tiptoed to the front of the store just in time to see Lydia Malone come giggling through the door with another girl.

"Hey, Brandi," said Lydia to her friend, "remember when we used to collect china horses? How dumb was that?" Lydia leaned against the jewelry counter.

"Speaking of dumb," replied Brandi. She cocked her head in the direction of Robby.

Robby had paused in front of a basket of polished stones. "'Good-luck stones,'" he was saying slowly, reading a card attached to the basket. "'Fifty cents each.' Fifty cents! Uh-oh. That's too much. Margaret! I'm almost out of money!" Robby bounced on his toes.

At the front of the store, Brandi dissolved in laughter. "What a retard!" she exclaimed, and bounced up and down.

"*Shh!*" hissed Lydia. "Shut up! My sister's here. Get out of the store."

Lydia pushed Brandi through the door. Ruby, wincing, turned to look at Robby.

Robby's gaze remained on the basket of stones. He dropped the blue one he'd been examining back into the basket, and then, eyes still on the stones, he dissolved into loud tears. He cried the way Ruby used to cry when she was very little and very tired. He drew in a deep breath and sobbed.

"Good heavens. What on earth is the matter here?" asked Mrs. Grindle, hurrying down the aisle to Robby. Ruby thought she looked supremely irritated.

"Sorry, Mrs. Grindle," said Margaret. "Robby's just a little upset. Robby, are you ready to pay for your things?"

"No, I am not ready!"

"Hey, Robby, want a piece of gum?" asked Ruby, pulling a stick of Juicy Fruit out of her pocket.

"No! And I am not a retard!"

"Look, Robby," said Margaret. "How about this little whale? I'll get it for you. You —"

"I AM NOT A RETARD!"

Margaret put her arms around Robby. "That was a horrible thing to say," she agreed.

"It is a *sensitive subject* and that person ought to know better," wailed Robby.

Ruby found herself backing away, backing down the aisle toward the door. When she reached the checkout counter, she noticed Nikki, now engrossed in a display of colored pencils. She seemed unaware of

Robby, and Ruby felt an unexpected pang of jealousy. Nikki wasn't bothered by Robby's crying and shouting. But Ruby was. She couldn't help herself. And so she hurried out of the store, without saying good-bye to Margaret or Robby.

CHAPTER 16

The Missing Necklace

Nikki Sherman picked up a box of pencils from the shelf in Stuff 'n' Nonsense. She looked through the little window in the box to see what colors were inside. Tropical shades, she thought. Very nice. But Nikki had not one penny with her. She set the box back.

The store had grown quiet. The big boy who had cried so loudly was gone. Nikki hadn't wanted to appear too curious about what was going on. She felt bad for the boy. Robby, she thought his name was. That horrible, tacky girl had come into the store with the other girl, whose father was a dentist, and she had called him a retard and of course Robby had gotten upset. What had the girl *thought* would happen?

Nikki had heard a third girl, a nice one, offer to buy Robby a toy of some sort, and a few minutes later, she and Robby had stood in front of the checkout counter, not far from Nikki.

"All right," the store owner had said with a fierce glance at Robby. "What have you got here?"

Robby spread his items on the counter. He wiped his nose with the back of his hand (which made the store owner cringe and look pointedly at a box of Kleenex) and said, "I added and added and I know I have enough."

"Well, let me ring you up," said the lady impatiently. Her fingers clacked away at the register and she said, "That comes to one dollar and seventy-nine cents."

"With tax?" asked Robby.

"With tax."

"I did it! I did it, Margaret. Look. All those stickers and two tattoos and the little parachute man. All those *fragile* things and I still have some money left over. I did a good job today."

"You certainly did," replied Margaret.

Nikki marveled that Robby seemed to have forgotten the cruel words that had upset him so — although she had been called many cruel words herself and remembered how quickly she could sweep them to the back of her brain when she needed to.

Robby pushed his money across the counter and the lady handed him his change and a paper bag, his purchases tucked inside. Then, hand in hand, Robby and Margaret left Stuff 'n' Nonsense.

Nikki abandoned the pencils and charcoals and edged to the jewelry counter. She let out a small sigh and looked at the clock over the door. Another half an hour before the old bat's class would end. What was Nikki supposed to do? She didn't want to sit around with Olivia and Flora and Ruby again, but she had no money and didn't feel like looking in stores any longer.

Nikki let out a larger sigh, left Stuff 'n' Nonsense, and crossed the street to Needle and Thread. She opened the door, the bell jangling above her. Sure enough, Mrs. DuVane's class was still in progress. Nikki could see eight heads bent over embroidery hoops and a basket of silk ribbon in the center of the table. Sitting at another table, all alone, was the old lady who was often working away at a pile of mending. On the couch, huddled over some large pieces of brightly colored fabric, were Olivia and Flora. They didn't look up from their work, but Ruby, who was watching them, did glance at her. And Nikki, tired of always arguing with the girls (feeling contrary used up a lot of energy, she realized), smiled at Ruby. Ruby offered a small smile in return.

Nikki was about to settle on the couch next to Ruby when the door to Needle and Thread blasted open behind her, and in charged the lady who owned Stuff 'n' Nonsense. The look on her face was angry — so angry that Nikki, surprised, lost her balance and stumbled onto the couch, nearly landing in Ruby's lap.

What on earth was the matter with the lady? Nikki

and Ruby looked at each other, and Nikki could read fear on Ruby's face.

Flora and Olivia looked up, too, and Olivia said, "Mrs. Grindle? What's wrong?"

Mrs. Grindle ignored Olivia. She stepped toward Nikki, held out her hand, and said loudly, "Give it back, please."

Nikki said nothing. Give what back? She glanced helplessly from Ruby to Olivia to Flora.

"Gina?" Gigi left the class and approached Mrs. Grindle, followed closely by Mrs. DuVane and Min. "What's going on?"

"This young *lady*," replied Mrs. Grindle in a tone implying that she thought Nikki was anything but a lady, "just stole a necklace from my store."

"What?" cried Nikki. She held out her hands, indicating that they were empty. "I — I — where would I put a necklace? I don't have a purse. I don't even have any pockets."

"All I know," said Mrs. Grindle, "is that you were just in my store, and I had just put a new necklace in the display by the door. You left, and now the necklace is gone."

Nikki shrugged. "I still don't have it."

"Well, then you hid it somewhere."

"I did not!"

Ruby stood up. "I was sitting right here when Nikki came in the store, and she didn't hide anything."

"Maybe you just didn't see her hide it."

"Why don't you search our store?" suggested Ruby.

"Ruby! Don't be impertinent," said Min.

"But, Min, this isn't fair," spoke up Flora.

"Yeah, Mrs. Grindle's just accusing Nikki because Nikki is a kid and Mrs. Grindle is a grown-up," said Olivia, "and she thinks she can get away with it."

"Olivia!" exclaimed Gigi. "Please apologize to Mrs. Grindle."

"Sorry, Mrs. Grindle," said Olivia, who didn't sound sorry at all.

Nikki hung her head and her eyes took in her clothes, which she knew were not at all what Mrs. DuVane had hoped she would wear on her trips into town. Too-small flip-flops, thin T-shirt that had once been white but was now a faint shade of gray and pocked with tiny holes in both front and back, and shorts that were too big and a boy's besides, since they had once belonged to Tobias. Then there were Nikki's hands, which were gray with dirt. Nikki raised her eyes to Mrs. Grindle and thought she knew the real reason she was being accused of stealing.

"I'm going to ask you one more time, young lady," said Mrs. Grindle fiercely. "Did you take that necklace?"

Nikki stepped directly in front of Mrs. Grindle. "No. I did not. I don't steal."

Mrs. Grindle stared at Nikki for a few moments. Then she said, "I don't know whether you are telling the truth, but from now on you are to stay away from my store." She turned around, stalked out of Needle and Thread, and made her way across Main Street.

Nikki, her face burning, whispered to Mrs. DuVane, "Can we go home now, please?"

CHAPTER 17

The Barbecue

Early on the afternoon of the Row House party, Ruby and Flora sat on their front stoop, waiting for Min to come home from a doctor's appointment. Ruby regarded the houses across the street, large wooden homes painted muted shades of mustard and green and tan, dating back to the mid-1800s.

"Min wasn't even born when those houses were built," said Ruby thoughtfully.

"Min's *parents* weren't even born," said Flora.

"Everything is old here."

"Everything is different here."

Ruby sniffed at the heavy August air and watched a chickadee land on the branch of a maple tree. "I kind of like it, though. . . . *Kind* of."

"Mmm."

"Do you think it's okay to like it even though Mom and Dad aren't here?"

"I don't know. I guess so." Flora looked at her watch. "Min should be back by now. I wonder what the doctor said about her wrist."

Ruby didn't answer. She sat with her chin in her hands for several moments, then said, "I can't believe Mrs. Grindle banned Nikki from her store. Why wouldn't she believe her? Is it just because Nikki's family doesn't have much money? I hate people like that."

"Don't hate," said Flora. "That makes you the same kind of person as Mrs. Grindle."

"Well, anyway, you know what we have here? A *mystery*," said Ruby dramatically. "A true mystery." She narrowed her eyes. "And here's the big question: If Nikki didn't take the necklace, who did?"

"Tell me again who was in the store when you were there with Robby and Margaret," said Flora.

"Well, Mrs. Grindle and Nikki, of course. Nikki was looking at art supplies," replied Ruby. "And Lydia came into the store for a few minutes with some friend of hers. The two of them were mean to Robby. And there were a couple of people in the back of the store, but I don't know who they were."

"Hmm. And when did Mrs. Grindle think she had put out the necklace? Maybe it was earlier than she remembers, before any of you were even in the store."

"Ooh, that's good, Flora," said Ruby admiringly.

"You're thinking like a real detective. Hey, look, there's Min!" Ruby jumped to her feet. "Let's see if she got her cast off yet."

Min, who had walked home from her appointment on Main Street, was still wearing the cast, but she was wearing a smile, too. "The doctor said everything is healing nicely and the cast can come off next week. He also said I can drive again."

Flora thought about the last few weeks when Min hadn't been allowed to drive. Because Camden Falls was small, and because Min had such good friends and neighbors, this hadn't been much of a problem, certainly not as much of a problem as it would have been in Flora and Ruby's old town. Here, Min and the girls could walk to Main Street, and the Row House neighbors had shopped for their groceries and driven them on any long-distance errands. Still, Flora had felt vulnerable. Now as she watched her grandmother cross the front yard, her purse and mail clutched in her good arm, she said, "Min? What if you had broken your leg when you fell? What would we have done?"

"Sweetie," Min interrupted her, "let's not talk about the what-ifs right now."

"But, really, what if —"

"Flora," said Min, "I know things aren't perfect for us. But I'm working on that. I'm going to make sure you and Ruby are always taken care of. I promise. Right now, it's time to get ready for the barbecue. It's going to be a fun afternoon. Try to enjoy it."

"But," said Flora, "what if —"

"Flora!" Ruby exclaimed suddenly. "We forgot to wrap the prizes! The prizes for the games this afternoon. We'd better go get Olivia. We have to get the stuff for the races, too. The egg, the spoon, the sack . . ."

"And I have pies to finish," said Min.

Flora's mind was still stuffed with questions. What if Min got sick and couldn't work at Needle and Thread anymore? Could she afford to retire? What if Min got sick and couldn't take care of her granddaughters? What would happen to Ruby and Flora then?

"Flora? Come *on!*" said Ruby, stamping her foot.

Flora had a little talk with herself. Bad thoughts begone, she said silently. Get out of my head. I don't need you here. You are not useful. "Okay," she said to Ruby a moment later. "Let's go."

Ruby headed for the kitchen door. "Let's leave this way," she said. "I want to look in everyone's backyards. I want to see if people are getting ready yet."

Flora looked at Ruby's hopeful face and remembered the times when her parents had been busy or distracted or tired but had still managed to attend Ruby's performances or plan birthday parties or sit down to play board games. So she set aside her worries and took Ruby's hand as they stepped through the kitchen door.

"Look! People *are* getting ready!" said Ruby.

In the yards of the Row Houses, checked tablecloths and extra chairs and ice-filled tubs of sodas were appearing. Dr. Malone had placed stereo speakers in his windows, and the Fongs, as requested by Olivia, Flora, and Ruby, had cleared their yard so that the races and game playing could take place there. Through open windows, Flora could smell pies and roasted chicken and fresh bread and a new smell — one she hadn't encountered before this summer in Camden Falls — that she identified as cilantro. Flora skipped a little skip as she and Ruby approached Olivia's back door.

Two hours later, the barbecue was under way. Every single Row House resident had ambled into the backyards. Twenty-five people laughing and talking and calling to one another, turning their faces to the sunshine. The Morris girls wore sundresses made by their mother from fabric purchased at Needle and Thread. Robby wore a new yellow baseball cap, and to Flora's great surprise, Mr. Pennington wore shorts, sandals, and a Disney World T-shirt. From Dr. Malone's speakers floated various kinds of music, including Min's beloved Gershwin. Daisy Dear sat with Jacques under a picnic table, waiting for food to be dropped. Sweetie, the Willets' cat, stalked Twinkle and Bandit, the Malones' cats. Margaret and Robby sat together on a lawn chair, and Lydia, Ruby noted, sat sullenly by herself next to a bowl of potato chips, which she kept reaching into and finally pulled into her lap, her own personal private bowl of chips.

Ruby, standing a short distance away, considered Lydia. Here, she realized, was one of the suspects in her robbery case. A good detective would tail her suspect, Ruby thought. She watched Lydia for a solid five minutes, but all Lydia did was glower at people and eat potato chips.

The younger Row House children ran from yard to yard, shrieking and shouting, until Flora and Olivia convinced the kids to go to the Fongs' to play games. Ruby joined them.

When the food was brought out, the children slowed down and, clutching prizes they'd won at the games, milled from yard to yard, investigating the platters of chicken and ribs, the plates of fruit salad and watermelon slices, and later an array of cakes and cookies and pies.

Ruby filled her plate with food, started to sit down at a table with Flora and Olivia, then noted that her robbery suspect was two yards away. She carried her plate over to the Willets', where she sat on a bench and observed Lydia, who was perched on the handrail the Willets had installed along the two steps up to their back door. She was holding a hot dog in one hand, a cell phone in the other, and was chatting away. Ruby strained to listen, but all she heard were snatches of conversation that meant little to her: "Six o'clock tonight. Everyone will be there." "No, not Cheryl, *Megan*." "I don't know, my blue shirt, I guess."

Ruby lost interest, yawned, and turned her attention to her meal.

From a chair nearby, Mrs. Willet watched the afternoon unfold. Her brain was foggy and grew foggier every day. Months ago, Mrs. Willet had realized something was wrong. Back then, she knew she was getting foggy. But slowly, even that knowledge had disappeared, along with much of her memory. Now she simply felt the afternoon slip away, each moment passing like a car on a train, except that when the last car had zipped by, Mrs. Willet had no memory of the train.

Earlier, Mr. Willet had settled his wife in a wicker chair. He had brought her first a glass of lemonade, then a plate of chicken and salad, and later a saucer with two cookies on it. As she was finishing the cookies, he said to her, "Dear, we've planned something special for the end of the party. Something for Flora and Ruby. Do you remember who they are? They're right over there. See them? They're Min Read's granddaughters, the ones who moved here this summer. And we thought it would be fun to surprise them, to welcome them to Camden Falls."

Mrs. Willet said nothing. She watched as the cars on the train began to pass again. First that nice Mr. Pennington (she thought that was his name, but she wasn't sure) called all the neighbors into the Willets' yard. Then the girl whose name was probably Olivia motioned two unfamiliar girls to a bench. "You sit over there," Olivia said, and added, "I kept a really good secret from you! Everyone's going to welcome you to your new home. The Morrises will be first."

Before Mrs. Willet's weary eyes, the four Morris children put on a skit titled "New Neighbors" in which the younger kids pretended to be baby bears welcomed to a forest neighborhood by an elk and a fox, played by the twins.

Then Mr. and Mrs. Fong presented Ruby and Flora with handmade picture frames. "For old pictures you already have," said Mrs. Fong, "or new ones you haven't taken yet."

"I have something you can put in them!" said Robby. "These are pictures I drew myself. There's one of each family in the Row Houses, because you're our new neighbors, like the baby bears. Okay, Ruby, you take four pictures, and Flora, you take four. Even Steven."

Mrs. Willet sat quietly and watched as Mr. Pennington presented the girls with a copy of *Sounder*, telling them it was a story about bravery; as Margaret and Lydia, giggling (Ruby thought her suspect now looked disarmingly normal and not at all robber-like), sang a song they'd written called "This Town Is Your Town"; as the Walters gave the girls a certificate, carefully decorated by Olivia and her brothers, making the girls official Row House Residents; as Min Read, her good hand trembling and her mouth quivering, presented each of her granddaughters with a piece of jewelry that had belonged to their mother; and finally, as Mr. Willet (Mrs. Willet had a vague idea that this man might be her husband) gave the girls a small album of photos. "These pictures are of your mother and her sister when they were little girls and lived right here."

"Thank you," said Flora in a whisper, and Ruby knew her sister wanted to cry but refused to do so in front of all these people.

"Thank you," said Ruby, somewhat stiffly. Then she hugged Mr. Willet around his waist.

Mrs. Willet just watched. She watched Flora and Ruby accept their gifts, watched as the food was taken inside and chairs were folded and people called good-bye. When at last that man who might be her husband helped her out of her chair, she grinned at him and said, "Whose birthday party *was* this? I had a wonderful time."

Two doors away, Flora and Ruby sat in the kitchen with Min and spread their treasures across the table.

"That was an excellent surprise," said Ruby.

And Flora stood up to kiss Min's cheek.

CHAPTER 18

What Ruby Sees

"Ruby," said Min one afternoon when Mary Woolsey had arrived at Needle and Thread and settled herself at her worktable, "could you please run across the street and ask Mrs. Grindle if she has any aspirin? We've run out of it and Mary has a headache."

"Why didn't she take an aspirin before she left her house?" said Ruby, who not only didn't want to face Mrs. Grindle but was having a bad day, which had started when she had fallen out of bed that morning and later tripped over the living room rug.

Min raised her eyebrows at Ruby. "May I remind you that getting your allowance is contingent on doing your chores, and that one of your chores is helping out at the store? Do you know what 'contingent' means?"

"It means I won't get my allowance if I don't go across the street to that evil old —"

"Ruby! We do not speak like that. Please apologize and then go calm down. I'll ask Flora or Olivia to run across the street."

"Sorry," muttered Ruby. Then she stalked out of the store, calling over her shoulder, "I'm going to take a walk." She looked at Stuff 'n' Nonsense and stuck out her tongue, hoping Mrs. Grindle would see her.

Ruby stomped past Zack's and then Heaven, the jewelry store, before she began to feel calmer. She slowed down and crossed the street to Time and Again, where she paused to peer in the window at the rows of used books on display. The children's books were on the left, and in the front was a copy of *The Cat Ate My Gymsuit*, by Paula Danziger. It was on sale for seventy-five cents, but Ruby had only a quarter in her pocket.

Ruby wandered into Frank's Beans and breathed in the aroma of coffee and chocolate and vanilla beans.

"Hi, Frank," she greeted the man behind the cash register.

"Hey there, Ruby. How's it going?"

"Okay. How's business?"

Frank had opened the coffee shop not long before Flora and Ruby had arrived in Camden Falls. "Oh, it's perking along. Get it? Perking?" said Frank.

Ruby didn't, but she smiled anyway.

"Would you like a chocolate milk?" asked Frank. "It's on the house."

"Sure!" said Ruby, and she settled into a tall chair and looked out onto Main Street while she sipped her milk. She waved to Sonny, and then to Dr. Malone, who was returning to his dental office.

"Thanks, Frank," Ruby called later as she dropped her cup in the trash. "Come into Needle and Thread sometime and we'll give you a free . . . um, a free . . ."

Frank waved her off. "No need, Ruby, but it's a nice offer. Have a good day!"

Ruby popped in at the post office and called hello to Jackie and Donna, who were busy weighing packages. She chatted with Sharon, who was decorating the window of the Cheshire Cat. Finally, she found herself standing outside Zinder's. The day had grown unbearably hot, and Ruby's hair stuck damply to her forehead and neck. She was about to open the door, looking forward to a blast of air-conditioning, when she saw Lydia Malone disappear inside Bubble Gum. Ruby drew in her breath. Then she hurried along the sidewalk and followed Lydia into the store.

"Hi, Ruby!" said Mrs. Cooper, who was showing sample nail polish to a customer. "Let me know if you need any help."

Ruby winced. A good detective should do her tailing in secret. She waved a thank-you to Mrs. Cooper, then slipped down the nearest aisle in search of Lydia, but she saw no one. She headed for the aisle with the magical makeup — the makeup that glittered — longing for the day when Min would allow her to wear glitter nail polish. But again, no Lydia.

Ruby had picked up a bottle of polish called Heavenly Daze and had turned it over to check the price (just in case it was on sale for less than a quarter) when she saw Lydia in the next aisle, saw her right through Mrs. Cooper's backless shelves. Lydia didn't see Ruby, though, and Ruby watched her in silence, holding her breath.

Lydia picked up a tube of mascara, a tube of eyeliner, a bottle of blush. She set each item back on the shelf.

This game of detective was silly, Ruby said to herself. She was acting like a little kid playing make-believe.

And that was when Lydia picked up a compact, glanced across the store at Mrs. Cooper, who was still busy with the customer, and dropped the compact into the pocket of her shorts. Then, humming tunelessly, she walked out of the store in an impressively nonchalant manner.

Ruby's mouth dropped open.

She dashed around to the display of compacts and picked one up. The price tag read $39.

"Thirty-ni —" Ruby started to exclaim, then clapped her hand over her mouth.

Lydia had shoplifted after all, and she had shoplifted something expensive.

Ruby hurried out of the store. She looked up and down Main Street, but she didn't see Lydia.

Now what? Ruby knew she should probably tell Mrs. Cooper what she'd seen, but she didn't know Mrs. Cooper well and didn't want to sound like a tattletale. Min was the one she should talk to, of course. She began to hurry back to Needle and Thread. But Ruby was still mad at Min about the argument over Mrs. Grindle. And Min was probably still cross with Ruby. What if Min didn't believe her? She might think Ruby had invented a big story in order to make her forget she had taken away Ruby's allowance.

Ruby paused, then stood on the sidewalk for so long, trying to figure out what to do, that Jackie stuck her head out of the post office and said, "Everything all right, Ruby?"

Ruby nodded. She crossed Main Street and headed for Needle and Thread again. She planned to talk to Olivia. Olivia would believe her. Also, Olivia had not said to her, "First day with your new feet?" which was what Flora had said when Ruby tripped over the rug that morning.

"Olivia, I have to talk to you," Ruby said in an urgent whisper when she had returned to the store.

"Let me just finish unpacking this box," said Olivia.

"No, this is important!" Ruby's voice rose to a squeal.

"Okay, okay." Olivia stood up.

"Come to the back of the store with me."

Ruby and Olivia huddled by the worktable where the embroidery class would soon be held.

"What *is* it?" asked Olivia.

Ruby took a deep breath. "I just saw Lydia Malone steal something from Bubble Gum. I saw her with my own eyes. I swear."

"You swear? You're really not kidding?"

Ruby crossed her heart. "I wouldn't kid about something like this. I saw her drop a compact or whatever you call it into her pocket. It was an expensive one. I checked the price."

"And you're sure it was Lydia Malone?"

"Positive."

"Wow."

"Um, excuse me," said a voice from behind Ruby.

Ruby and Olivia whirled around to find themselves facing Nikki Sherman. "What —" Olivia began to say.

"I'm sorry to interrupt you," said Nikki quickly, "but I couldn't help overhearing you. The girl you were talking about, Lydia Malone — is she older than us? With short brown hair? Her father's a dentist?"

"Yes," said Olivia.

"Well . . . okay, she was in Stuff 'n' Nonsense the day Mrs. Grindle said I took that necklace from her store. She was with another girl, and the girl teased that boy Robby."

"I know," said Ruby.

"What's going on?" asked Flora, who had been working the cash register for Min and Gigi.

Olivia told her about Lydia. When she finished, the four girls looked at one another. It was Olivia who said finally, in hushed tones, "So I'll bet it was Lydia who stole the necklace after all. Lydia's . . . a shoplifter."

"We have to tell Min and Gigi," said Flora. "And we have to do it right now."

"Gigi just started teaching the class," said Olivia. "Tell Min, Flora."

"No, you tell her. You've known Lydia longer than I have. It'll mean more if you tell her."

So the girls gathered around Min, and Olivia told her what had happened.

"Lord love a duck!" exclaimed Min.

Later, after the class had ended, Min told Gigi the news, and to everyone's surprise, Gigi said, "You know, I thought I saw Lydia take a spool of thread the other day."

"From *our* store?" cried Ruby.

"Yes," said Gigi, "but I wasn't sure, and anyway, this isn't the sort of thing I'd expect from Lydia. She's always been such a nice girl. Ruby, let me ask you one more time: Are you certain about what you saw today?"

"Positive."

"All right then," said Min. "It's decided. We'll have to talk to Dr. Malone."

Nikki, who had said little that afternoon, looked

from one person to the next in awe. They were sticking up for her, and they barely knew her. They were sticking up for Nikki Sherman, with her stained T-shirt and rat's nest hair and uneven skirt.

Sticking up for her.

That almost never happened to a Sherman.

CHAPTER 19

The Truth Comes Out

"I wish I could come with you," whispered Olivia to Flora and Ruby as they followed Min and Gigi down Main Street. They had just closed up Needle and Thread for the day and the adults were going to talk to Dr. Malone. "I'm dying to know what happens."

Arm in arm, Min and Gigi walked briskly in front of the girls, their heads bent together, talking quietly.

"Are you sure you have to go with your parents?" asked Flora.

"Yes," replied Olivia. "We're going over to my other grandparents' house for dinner. I can't tell Mom and Dad I want to stay home and eavesdrop with you."

"No, I guess not," said Flora.

"You have to promise to tell me *everything* that happens. And I mean every single little detail."

"We promise," said Ruby.

"And remember to call Nikki. You said you'd tell her what happens, too."

"I'll remember." Ruby sounded impatient. "Now listen — here's what we're going to do. As soon as Min and Gigi are inside the Malones' house, we're going to get glasses from the kitchen — big drinking glasses should do it — and put them against the living room wall so we can listen to what goes on in the Malones' living room. If we —"

"*Shh!*" hissed Flora. "Keep your voice down. You know Min wouldn't approve of eavesdropping."

Ruby barely heard her sister. "Olivia, are you sure the Malones' living room is right on the other side of ours?"

Olivia nodded. "I know these houses inside and out. Once I made a blueprint of all the Row Houses. That was when I wanted to be an architect."

When Min and Gigi and the girls reached the Row Houses, Min said, "Okay, Flora and Ruby, you go on home now. Gigi and I are going to talk with Dr. Malone."

"Okay," said Flora. And Olivia said, "See you tomorrow, Gigi."

Flora and Ruby made a dash for the front door of their house, ran inside, found glasses in the kitchen, and flew into the living room. They rested the open end of each glass against the wall and pressed their ears to the other end.

"I can't hear anything," said Ruby after a few moments.

"Me, neither," said Flora.

"Maybe they're talking in the kitchen."

"Hey, I just thought of something!" cried Flora suddenly. "If the Malones' house is the opposite of ours — if the rooms that are on the left in our house are on the right in theirs and vice versa, then Lydia's room should be on the other side of mine. Quick! Bring your glass upstairs! Maybe we can hear Lydia talking to Margaret. Or maybe Lydia has figured out what's going on and she's panicked and called a friend."

"Flora, you're a genius!" said Ruby. The girls ran to Flora's bedroom with their glasses.

The wall dividing Lydia's room from Flora's was the wall against which Flora had placed her bed. The rest of the wall was taken up by the cedar wardrobe.

"On the bed!" ordered Ruby.

"Okay, but keep your stinky feet off my pillow."

"I think I can hear something," said Ruby breathlessly, kneeling at the foot of Flora's bed. "Yup, I definitely hear voices. But I can't make out any words."

Flora stood up. "All right, I'm going to go into the wardrobe. Maybe I can hear better from there." She scrambled off the bed, turned the key in the wardrobe latch, and wedged herself onto a shelf. Below her were two big drawers, which she had filled with her art and sewing supplies. Above her were the hangers for her clothes. Flora was shoving aside shoes and sweaters, wondering if she could actually sit in the wardrobe, when she heard the crackle of paper. She frowned. "Ruby?" she called. "Was that you?"

"What? *Shh!* Be quiet! Now I can hear two voices."

Flora felt around the dark shelf of the wardrobe. Her fingers identified objects as they met them: sneaker, sweatshirt, sandal, pom-pom sweater. And then they closed over what felt like a wad of paper. What was this? Flora hadn't put any papers in the wardrobe.

Flora slid off the shelf and examined what was in her hand. It was a packet of old pages that had been torn from a spiral notebook, each page filled with large looping handwriting. Flora sank down until she was sitting on the rug, leaning against the end of her bed, and began to read the first page:

Being the Personal Private Diary of Frannie Read (KEEP OUT — this means you, Allie)

Flora caught her breath. Frannie Read. That was her mother. And Allie was her aunt Allie, her mother's younger sister. This diary had been kept by Flora's mother.

October 10th — Monday. Back to school. Walked with Wendy.

Wendy, thought Flora. That must have been Olivia's mother, who lived next door even back then. Flora paused to consider her mother and Olivia's mother walking to school together, giggling and sharing secrets.

Allie wouldn't leave us alone, the diary continued. *Wendy and I wanted to talk about John Giancomo, who we THINK kissed Missy Truman at Pat's party. But it's possible he kissed someone's arm. It was so dark.*

Flora didn't know whether to laugh or to cry. Her mother's own personal diary! In her handwriting! Flora flipped through it. Page after page of sprawling words, occasionally illustrated with a drawing of a flower or a peace symbol. Flora tried to guess how old her mother had been when she had written these pages. She found months and dates listed but no year. Flora guessed she was twelve. Twelve or thirteen.

Flora glanced from the pages in her hand to the dark recesses of the wardrobe. Her mother's diary here in her mother's old room, the room in which Flora now slept.

"Ruby!" said Flora. "Come here. You really have to see this."

Ruby abandoned her glass and sat on the floor with her sister. "What is it?"

"An old diary of Mom's. Look."

The girls bent over the pages and read about the autumn of whatever year their mother had been documenting.

Wendy and I closed ourselves in my room this morning, another entry began. *We had to lock the door to keep Allie out. What a pest. Every time we mention boys, she asks us if we're going to marry them and then makes these kissing noises.*

"She and Olivia's mom were best friends," said Ruby.

"And she and Aunt Allie drove each other crazy," added Flora.

"Ew!" squealed Ruby as she turned to a new page. "Mom really did kiss a boy! I can't read about that!" She leaped onto the bed and held the glass to the wall again.

But Flora remained on the floor with the pages in her lap. She knew, of course, that her mother had grown up here. And she was aware that this had been her mother's room. But it wasn't until now, with her mother's words in front of her, her mother's voice in her head, that Flora understood that she, Flora Marie Northrop, belonged here. There was a place for her in this room, in this house, in this town. She could feel her Camden Falls roots reaching out to her.

For some reason this both comforted and frightened her, and she jumped up to stuff Frannie Read's diary back into the corner of the wardrobe. Then she shut the door with a bang and joined Ruby on the bed.

Ten minutes later, glasses still to the wall, Ruby and Flora were startled to hear the front door open and Min call, "Girls?"

"We're upstairs!" Flora replied.

"Quick! Hide the glasses!" said Ruby in a loud whisper.

The glasses had been safely stowed in Flora's dresser by the time Min appeared in the doorway.

"What happened?" Ruby asked.

"Well," said Min, looking serious (and also, thought Flora, very tired), "Gigi and I talked to Dr. Malone. He was upset, of course, but actually not surprised. He said he suspected that something was going on with Lydia. He just didn't know what. He's going to talk with her this evening."

Flora, who felt sad for the Malones, couldn't help also feeling relieved. She sent Ruby a secret smile, thinking of the happy phone call they could make to Nikki.

Not long after Flora and Ruby and Min had finished their dinner that night, when the crickets were tuning up for their loud nighttime symphony and the open windows admitted a damp breeze that turned Flora's dark hair into wispy curls, the telephone rang.

Min answered it, and as soon as Ruby heard her say, "Yes, Roger," she ran to Flora's room and exclaimed, "Dr. Malone is on the phone! I bet he talked to Lydia. I wonder how much trouble she's in."

"Ruby," said Flora, "you don't have to sound so excited."

"I can't help it. I solved the crime! Well, we did. And we got Nikki *out* of trouble, even if we got Lydia into it. It *is* exciting. Come on. Let's go downstairs."

Min hung up the phone in the kitchen and turned to see her granddaughters. "My stars," she said. "That was Dr. Malone. He had a long talk with Lydia, and Ruby, you were right. Lydia admitted to shoplifting the compact, along with the necklace, the thread, and a number of other things. Dr. Malone sounds shaken. He said Lydia's having a hard time right now and missing her mother. She's at a difficult age, too. Still, that's no excuse for her behavior. She's committed a crime, after all. Dr. Malone is going to see to it that she tells Mrs. Grindle what she did, that she apologizes to Nikki, that she returns the items she stole, and that she pays the shopkeepers back for any items she can't return. Hopefully, none of the shopkeepers will want to prosecute her for shoplifting. I'm more interested in seeing her get straightened out. Dr. Malone's going to make sure she finds a job to occupy her for the next few weeks until school starts. He doesn't want her to have so much time on her hands. She needs to earn money to pay everyone back, anyway."

"Wow," said Flora.

"Ruby," said Min, "I'm glad you told Gigi and me what you saw. You did the right thing. I think the Malones will work out their problems, even though they're having a tough time."

"Gosh," said Ruby as she and Flora climbed the stairs to their bedrooms later that night. "Maybe I *should* become a detective."

"Maybe," said Flora, whose mind was still on her mother's diary — and also on the box she'd found in the attic. She had forgotten about the box until, holding the creased pages of the diary that afternoon, she had once again found herself peeking into a long-ago life. Flora retreated to her room and waited until Ruby had closed her door for the night. Then she crept into the attic, hauled the box of papers out from under the eaves, and wrestled it down the stairs and into her room, where she shoved it as far under her bed as she could reach. For reasons she didn't understand, she wanted the box to be her secret.

CHAPTER 20

Wheels

One morning when Flora awoke, she stretched out in her bed and realized she was chilly. "King," she called to the cat curled by her head, "go lie on my feet. *Brr.*" Flora sniffed the air. "Autumn," she murmured. "It smells like autumn already." And it was, she realized with a start, almost the end of August. Summer vacation would soon be over. The Row House party had come and gone. Min's wrist was nearly healed. The necklace mystery had been solved and Lydia had found a job — she was now Robby's full-time sitter. Flora and Ruby had been living in Camden Falls for two months, and in a few days, school would start. Another beginning for Ruby and me, Flora thought. A new school year in a new school with new kids and new teachers. But not all new kids, she reminded herself. Olivia would be there. Nikki, too. Not every face would be unfamiliar.

Later that day, Flora and Olivia spread out their butterfly on a worktable at Needle and Thread. Flora was explaining to Olivia how to turn a curved seam ("Before you turn the fabric right side out, trim the seam to about a quarter of an inch and clip along the curve, right to the stitching, but not through it") when the bell over the door rang and in walked Nikki Sherman, looking cheerful.

"Hi!" she called.

Flora and Olivia abandoned the butterfly. "Hi!" they replied, surprised but pleased to see Nikki without Mrs. DuVane, who hadn't been in the store since the embroidery class had ended.

"How did you get here?" asked Olivia.

Nikki grinned. "On my bicycle. I never had a bicycle of my own, and then this morning Tobias — that's my brother — he said to come outside, and there was a bicycle waiting for me in the yard. It isn't new; Tobias found it at the dump. But he fixed it all up and made it run perfectly, so now I have wheels! I can come into town anytime I want."

"Nikki, that's great," said Flora.

Nikki glanced around the store. "Where's Ruby?" she asked.

"Running an errand for Min," Flora replied. "She'll be right back."

"Guess what," said Nikki.

"What?" said Olivia and Flora.

"Last week our phone rang — it doesn't always work, but it's working now — and I answered it and it was Lydia Malone. She was calling to say she was sorry about getting me in trouble over the necklace. And then the next day *Mrs. Grindle* called and *she* apologized, too."

"You're kidding," said Olivia.

"Nope." Nikki crossed her heart. "I still don't think I'll ever go in her store again, though."

"Me, neither," agreed Flora. "Not after what she did to you."

"She's a big meanie," added Olivia. "She always has been."

"At least she apologized," said Nikki.

Ruby returned a few minutes later, carrying a handful of mail and a bag from Camden Falls Art Supply. "Nikki!" she exclaimed. "What are you doing here?"

So Nikki repeated her story. When she finished, Ruby said, "*I'm* never going to Stuff 'n' Nonsense again, either. Min sent me there to get Post-its, but I got them at the art supply place instead."

"You guys?" said Nikki. "I have to say something to you. I mean, I want to say something. I want to say . . . I want to say that I'm really sorry I wasn't very nice before. You were nice to me, and, I don't know — -

coming here with Mrs. DuVane I felt kind of weird, and —"

"That's okay," said Flora. "It wasn't all your fault. We *weren't* always nice."

"I got whiney," said Ruby.

"I was bossy," added Olivia. "But let's just forget about that. Come on. Let's go sit down."

The girls settled onto the couches.

"You know what?" said Flora. "Weeks and weeks ago I had this idea about making teddy bears for kids who are having a bad time." She told Ruby and her friends about the article she'd seen and then she said to Olivia and Nikki, "After the accident, Ruby and I held onto our bears until someone came to take us home from the hospital."

"Min," said Ruby.

"Really? Not Annika's mother?" said Flora.

"No, it was Min."

"Well, it doesn't matter," said Flora. "The thing is that we held onto those teddies for dear life."

"Do you still have them?" asked Nikki.

"Definitely," said Ruby.

Flora was going to add that she slept with hers every night, but suddenly she wanted to keep that detail to herself.

"You know what?" said Olivia. "We could have a teddy bear workshop here at the store. If Gigi and

Min say it's all right, Needle and Thread could give a workshop for free and supply all the materials, too. The workshop could be for kids, and they would learn to sew by making the bears, and then the bears would be donated to kids who need them."

"That's a great idea!" said Nikki.

The girls were busy planning the workshop when Mary Woolsey entered the store.

"Hi," said Flora, Olivia, and Ruby.

Mary stood before them, looking weighed down by her layers of clothing, her necklace glinting in the overhead lights. She nodded to the girls, then made her way quietly to the table at the back of the store.

"Gosh, if Mary's here, it's later than I thought," said Flora. "You know what I want to do? I want to run home and check our mailbox. I sent off for this package of Halloween stencils, and I want to see if it came."

Flora dashed out of the store. Fifteen minutes later, she was back. "You guys!" she said. "The stencils aren't here, but guess what did come." She held out two white envelopes. "They're from Camden Falls Elementary. I bet they're our room assignments. Min, can we open these?" Flora handed the envelopes to her grandmother.

"Let's look at them together," said Min.

Min sliced open the envelopes with a pair of scissors, while Ruby, Olivia, Nikki, and Flora peered over her shoulder. "Let's see," said Min. "Ruby, it looks as though you'll be in Mr. Lundy's class, and Flora, you'll be in Mrs. Mandel's class."

"Ooh, you're lucky, Flora!" exclaimed Olivia. "Mrs. Mandel is the best teacher in the whole school. Everyone hopes to get her for sixth grade. I'm going to call Dad and see if my room assignment came, too."

Olivia grabbed the phone by the cash register, called her father, and then let out a whoop. "Yes!" she exclaimed. "I have Mrs. Mandel! Flora, we're going to be in the same class!"

"Maybe I should call home," said Nikki shyly. "Could I use your phone? I think Tobias is there." (Nikki's mother had headed for the welfare office that afternoon, Mae in hand. She said having Mae along was good luck because people always took pity on her.) "Tobias could check the mail."

Olivia, Flora, and Ruby crowded around Nikki while she made her phone call. When they heard her say, "You're kidding! I have Mrs. Mandel?" they cheered. (Ruby cheered more softly than the others, though, feeling left out of the Mrs. Mandel Club.)

Nikki stayed until closing time that afternoon, then said, "I'll see you tomorrow, now that I have wheels!" and she hopped on her bicycle and headed down Main Street, with Olivia, Ruby, and Flora waving to her as she pedaled away.

CHAPTER 21

The Photo

Flora recalled Augusts that were hot and steamy, day and night, with barely a breeze to stir the air. But here in Camden Falls, the end of August seemed to usher autumn in weeks before the calendar did. The days were warm enough for shorts and T-shirts, but by nightfall, cool air crept into the Row Houses and Min would say as she stood up from the table after dinner, "Land sakes, I believe I need a sweater."

It was on one of these cool evenings, with Min wearing her sweater and Flora and Ruby wearing sweatshirts over their nightgowns, that Flora's thoughts turned to the box hidden under her bed. She said good night to Min and her sister, kissed Daisy Dear on the nose, and hauled King Comma upstairs and into her room, where she shut the door. She retrieved the box, blowing dust bunnies off it, and climbed into bed. She had crawled under the covers with her teddy bear, and King was now purring in the tent under Flora's knees, when she also remembered her mother's diary. "Sorry, King Comma," said Flora. "I have to disturb you. I'll be right back." At last, settled in bed with both the box and the diary, Flora once again inched backward through the years. She turned first to the diary.

October 22nd — THE WEEKEND AT LAST!! Wendy and I are working on our Halloween costumes. We're going to be Raggedy Ann and Raggedy Andy, except that neither of us wants to be Raggedy Andy. Allie says she's coming trick-or-treating with us, but excuse me, did we invite her?

Flora smiled, then shut the diary. She laid it aside and opened the box, deciding to reach in with her eyes closed and see what she pulled out. Her fingers closed over what turned out to be a packet of letters, all written in a precise, tidy hand in faded blue ink, and all from someone named Martha to someone named Sophie.

Flora frowned. Martha. That was the name of Min's mother. And Sophie — was she Martha's sister, Min's aunt? Flora wondered how all these letters that had been written to Sophie had wound up back in Min's house. Oh, well. It didn't matter. Here they were, and Flora was eager to read them. Most of the letters were dated 1929 and 1930. Flora smoothed one out and rested it against her knees.

Oh, Sophie, this is terrible, the letter began. *Lyman has left his job. All those people — his clients, our* _friends_ *— have lost their fortunes. They blame Lyman, and this morning he told me he felt he couldn't continue to work. I didn't want to say his decision seems cowardly, but . . .*

What? What had happened? Flora placed the letters in chronological order and began to read. Very quickly, she pieced together a story about Min's parents from a time before Min was born — a story Flora had never heard. It seemed that Lyman Davis, Flora's great-grandfather, had been a stockbroker at a prestigious company in Camden Falls. Although still young, he had been one of the most trusted men in town in the 1920s and, Flora realized, probably one of the wealthiest. By investing people's money, he had made small (and sometimes large) fortunes for them and an enormous fortune for himself. He was highly sought after and had a long list of clients, which included many of the Davises' friends and a few family members as well.

Then, in October of 1929, the stock market crashed, and — overnight — all across the country people lost their entire savings. The United States was plunged into the Great Depression. In Camden Falls, many of Lyman's clients blamed him for their misfortune.

Was this true? wondered Flora. *Was* he partly to blame, even if the crash wasn't his fault?

Flora turned back to the letters. She learned that two weeks after the crash, unable to bear the strain, Lyman left his job and never returned to work. From what Flora could understand, this didn't affect his family much. Because of an inheritance of Martha's, they still had plenty of money to live on. Perhaps they didn't live quite as lavishly as before, but their lives changed only a little. The lives of many of Lyman's clients, however, changed dramatically.

Flora's eyes were growing heavy, and she set aside the letters. She reached into the box once more and this time pulled out a manila envelope. It was full of loose photos that appeared more recent than some of the other items in the box. Flora sifted through them, then came awake with a start when she realized she was looking at photos of two young girls who she thought were her mother and Olivia's mother. She turned one of them over. Sure enough, written on the back was *Frannie and Wendy, July 1976.* Flora smiled. She'd have to show these photos to Olivia.

"King Comma," said Flora, now fully awake, "I'm very sorry, but I have to disturb you again. I just thought of something." Flora slid out of her bed and opened the drawer of her desk in which she had put the picture frame given to her by the Fongs. She remembered that Mrs. Fong had said the frame was for an old photo Flora already had or for a new one not yet taken. But, Flora thought as she inserted one of the photos of her mother and Wendy into the frame, sometimes an old photo could also be a new one. Flora had a feeling she might see something new in this old picture every time she looked at it — and that she was forging the next link in the chain that connected her to her mother and to Camden Falls.

Flora set the frame on the desk. Then she returned to her bed. She was making a pile of photos to show Olivia, when she found a small photo, slightly older than the others, of her mother at about age four posing with a familiar-looking woman. Flora checked the back of the photo. It was labeled *Frannie and Mary — 1970.* So this was her mother at age four, but who was Mary? Min's sister, Mary Elizabeth? Probably. Mary Elizabeth would have been her mother's aunt.

Flora's eyes were closing again. She gathered up the papers and photos on her bed, set aside the pictures of Wendy, and returned the other things to the box. She was about to slide the box under her bed when she retrieved the photo of her mother and Mary. There was something about the photo, something . . . what was it? It nagged at Flora. She studied her mother and the woman again, checked the writing on the back again. Nothing came to her, but the nagging feeling wouldn't go away.

At last, Flora slipped the photo into the drawer of her bedside table and turned out her light. Her dreams that night were unsettled.

CHAPTER 22

Nighttime

If you were to walk the country roads west of Main Street in Camden Falls, Massachusetts, on a rainy evening in early September, you might eventually come to an isolated house off the main road. The drive leading to this house is rutted, and the ruts are filling with chilly rain. The drive seems long, especially in the growing dark, and the only noises to be heard are outdoor, nighttime noises — a few brave crickets calling, the sudden barking of dogs, an early owl out hunting, twigs snapping under your feet as you trudge along. At the end of this drive is a sad-looking house, small and drooping, but with signs of care, too. Flowers have been planted by the front stoop, the steps have been swept clean, and a wreath of dried roses has been hung on the door.

Now take a peek through the windows. There is Nikki Sherman reading *James and the Giant Peach* to

Mae. The sisters are snuggled together on a couch that's full of holes, but they don't mind because they have traveled to another land and their thoughts are with James and the peach. The house is quiet for once, and Nikki is grateful. Her father is out (Nikki doesn't care where, as long as he's out), Tobias is in one of the sheds working on a car, and Mrs. Sherman is in the kitchen. She's humming, which means she's happy, which means Nikki and Mae are happy, too. Nikki is also happy because for the first time in her life she has friends. Three of them.

Turn away from the Shermans now, travel back to Main Street, and soon you'll find yourself on Aiken Avenue. There are the Row Houses with mist twining around the corners and rooftops, a few damp maple leaves squishing beneath your feet. You'll see that most of the windows have been closed to keep out the damp, and since it isn't too late, lights are on in many of those windows. Through one of the open windows, music can be heard.

Take a peek inside the house at the north end of the row. There are the Fongs, sitting together on one kitchen chair, both trying to talk on the phone at the same time. They have just found out wonderful news, and they are calling all their relatives to pass it along.

"Dad!" exclaims Barbara Fong. "Marcus and I are going to have a baby!"

Marcus leans into the phone and adds, "You're going to be a grandfather!"

When they finish their call, they dial another number right away.

At the other end of the Row Houses, the Morris children are trying on last year's school clothes. The twins' outgrown clothes are being passed down to the smaller children. "I'll never get anything but hand-me-downs!" wails Travis. "Because I'll always be smaller than Mathias." Alyssa adds, "Only Lacey and Mathias get new clothes. No fair!" And their mother says, "For heaven's sakes, you're all going to get new shoes tomorrow."

In the Malones' house, Lydia has closed herself in her room and is playing music at top volume. She's lying on her bed, totaling up the money she has earned so far by baby-sitting for Robby. She has already returned as many of the stolen items as possible, and she has begun to repay the shopkeepers for the things she can't return, but she has a long way to go. Lydia sighs. She thinks about Robby. Baby-sitting for him hasn't been as bad as she thought it would be. In fact, she admits (but only to herself) that she really likes Robby. He was a sweet kid, and now he's a sweet teenager. Lydia pictures Brandi imitating Robby, and she cringes. Then she thinks about school. She hasn't seen Brandi since she began her sitting job, and that's been fine. But what will happen when school starts? She can't avoid Brandi forever.

Next door at the Willets', Mr. Willet is having another evening tussle with his wife. He has been talking to her for almost an hour now about brushing her teeth. And Mrs. Willet doesn't want to do it. Not because she doesn't want clean teeth, but because she isn't sure who this man is. He's a stranger in her house, and he wants her to brush her teeth, and this does not seem right. If only she could find her husband.

Three doors down, Olivia Walter is in bed, leafing through a book about snails, her bright fabric butterfly hanging on the wall above her bed. Her brothers are in their beds, also reading. Downstairs, her parents sit at the kitchen table, papers and bank statements spread before them. Mrs. Walter takes off her glasses, rubs her eyes, then rests her head in her hands.

Robby Edwards and his parents are also sitting in their kitchen, but their table is strewn with Robby's new school supplies. "You always have to have a pencil case," Robby is saying. "This one is perfect. And I have two erasers, five pencils, a three-ring notebook, the paper with the holes on the sides, and a ruler. Uh-oh! Where's my calculator? I need a calculator this year."

Next door, Mr. Pennington is getting ready to go to bed. He stands in the kitchen and walks around and around, making certain that the burners are turned off, that the refrigerator is tightly closed, that Jacques's water bowl is full, that no milk or anything that could spoil has been left out on the counter. He checks these things, then checks again. He makes sure the doors and windows are closed and locked. He plans to make a list of things to do each evening, so he can be sure nothing is amiss.

In the house that Flora and Ruby Northrop now share with their grandmother, Min sits before the television, smiling a little as she smocks an insert for a sample back-to-school dress she plans to display in Needle and Thread. Upstairs, Ruby is in bed and has turned off her light, but she isn't asleep. She's lying on her back, hands behind her head, daydreaming about the Camden Falls Children's Chorus for which she'll soon audition. Ruby imagines herself standing on risers with the other members of the chorus, singing "It's the Hard-Knock Life" from the musical *Annie*. Ruby will have a solo. She'll get to imitate Miss Hannigan and cry, "You stay up till this dump shines like the top of the Chrysler Building!" Ruby will put plenty of emphasis on the word *shines*, and everyone will laugh and clap when her part is over.

Across the hall, Flora's light is still on. Flora is in bed reading her mother's journal. This has been a year of changes, Flora reflects, many of them heartbreaking, and she knows more changes are to come. She hopes she's strong enough to face them.

Flora closes the diary and removes the photo of her

mother and Mary from the drawer in her bedside table. She studies it again. Something nags at her each time she looks at it. Flora goes over every detail in the photo. At last, her eyes light on the necklace around Mary's neck. Suddenly, Flora is certain she has seen that necklace somewhere before. She studies it. A tiny star hangs from the chain. Flora stares, then her mouth drops open. She knows where she's seen that necklace. She has seen it around the neck of Mary Woolsey. This isn't a photo of her mother with her aunt Mary Elizabeth. This is a photo of her mother with Scary Mary.

Flora drops the photo and feels goose bumps rise on her arms. She yanks open the drawer of the bedside table, thrusts the photo under a notebook, bangs the drawer shut, and turns off her reading light. She lies in bed for a long time, eyes wide open, as one by one, the other lights in the Row Houses blink off, and finally this block on Aiken Avenue in Camden Falls is dark.

Ann M. Martin

talks about

Main Street

Q: What inspired you to write Main Street?

A: When my editor, David, asked me if I'd be interested in working on another series, he tempted me with the idea of writing, in some way, about sewing, which is my favorite hobby. So I began to think about sewing, then sewing stores, then towns with sewing stores in them, and finally about small towns, which I love. I also was inspired by a British author whose books my mother used to love. The author is Dora Saint, and she wrote under the pen name Miss Read.

When I began to create the town of Camden Falls, the Miss Read stories were on my mind. Also, I had discovered while working on *A Corner of the Universe* and *Here Today* that I liked writing about a large cast of characters and creating a setting so important that it becomes a character itself.

Q: Is Camden Falls at all like the town in which you live?

A: I now live not far from the town of Woodstock, New York, and although if you compared a map of Woodstock with my map of Camden Falls you would find many differences, Woodstock is definitely the inspiration for Camden Falls, just as Tinker Street in Woodstock is the inspiration for Main Street. The two towns are not exactly the same, but there are many similarities. Both are very small, both are plunked down in hilly countryside, and many of Woodstock's town traditions are finding their way into Main Street.

Q: Are any of the characters in Main Street based on people you know?

A: Some of the characters are named after people I know. For instance, Min is named for the mother of one of my friends, who really is called Min by her granddaughter because she so often says, "In a minute." Mr. Pennington is loosely based on a friend of my father's, and the Willets are based on my own parents and their experiences after my mother was diagnosed with Alzheimer's. Sonny Sutphin is based on a man who was well known in the town of Princeton, New Jersey, when I was growing up there. He was wheelchair-bound and spent his days wheeling himself around town, selling candy from the tray of his chair. It was because of Sonny that I became addicted to Sky Bars in high school. Finally, Flora and Ruby are based on two sisters I know. The younger one is very much like Ruby. She loves to be onstage, has performed in community theatre, sings in a children's chorus, and takes dance lessons. The older one is quieter, more serious, and a bit introspective, and although she's not interested in sewing and crafts like Flora is, she does develop passionate interests.

Q: Which character in Main Street do you relate to the most?

A: Although I see bits of myself in many characters, I most relate to Flora. Flora's interests are mine, and so is her personality — quiet, shy, introspective, and as desperate to avoid the spotlight as Ruby is to seek it.

Q: Flora and Ruby have a very spirited relationship as sisters. What was your relationship with your sister Jane like when you were Flora's age?

A: While Flora and Ruby are based on the sisters I mentioned above, Jane's and my relationship was somewhat similar to theirs. Jane was far more outgoing than I was, enjoyed playing sports, and did have parts in several plays, but she did not share Ruby's interest in dance classes, children's chorus, and so forth (although my sister and I both very much enjoyed being taken to

Broadway shows). I, on the other hand, loved crafts, drawing, sewing, and knitting, hated sports, and was as shy as Jane was outgoing. Still, the two of us spent hours together creating imaginary worlds, writing plays and radio shows that we put on for our parents, and taking care of our many pets.

Q: Where did the idea come from to "peek in the windows" of the people in Camden Falls?

A: The town of Camden Falls has many interesting people in it (as does any town), and I wanted to be able to peek into the lives of more than just the main characters. Also, giving the reader a sense of the townspeople contributes to the feel of the town itself. The characters shape the town, the town shapes the characters, and details about the people reveal the world of Camden Falls.

Q: What were your favorite parts of town when you were growing up?

A: When I was growing up, we lived several miles from downtown Princeton, so I wasn't able to walk into town as Flora and Ruby and Olivia do, nor did I spend nearly as much time in town as they do. But Jane and I went into town fairly often with our parents. One of my favorite places was the public library, which was much smaller then than it is now, and one of my favorite stores was called the Hobby Shop, which was where we could buy paint and markers and pastels and craft supplies. Of course I loved Clayton's Yarn Shop, too. Then there was a very fancy French restaurant that we only went to for special occasions, and Hulit's, where we bought our new school shoes every September. If we were lucky, we might run into Sonny and convince our mother or father to buy candy or a Slim Jim from him.

Q: Sewing and crafts are very important to you. When did you start sewing? Who taught you?

A: My father's mother taught me to knit when I was about eight. Around the same time, my mother taught me to do needlepoint and crewel work. Later she taught me to sew. In high school I took sewing, and as an adult I've taken sewing classes, too. I taught myself to smock by reading a book.

My father is a cartoonist, and as a child I took lots of art and drawing classes. Our house was full of paint and paper and craft supplies.

Q: Now, what are your favorite things to make?

A: My favorite things to make are smocked dresses or outfits for my godchildren and my friends' and cousins' children. Sometimes I make embroidered dresses or try other sewing techniques. I do a lot of knitting, too, and I knit for my nephew.

Q: Flora and Ruby have a cat, King Comma, and Min has a dog, Daisy Dear. Do you have pets? Do you like dogs or cats or both?

A: I like both dogs and cats, although when I was growing up, we had only cats. I didn't get a dog until Sadie came into my life in 1998. So now I have Sadie, who's a mixed breed (she looks like a miniature golden retriever), and three cats, Gussie, Woody, and Willy. Also, I foster stray cats for a local animal rescue organization, so often I'm taking care of a temporary cat or two.

Q: If you were going to work at a store on Main Street, which one do you think it would be?

A: Definitely Needle and Thread. I've always wanted to work in a sewing store. It would be fun to work in one of the bookstores, too.

Continue your walk down down

Main Street

with

Needle and Thread

"I can't believe summer's over," said Olivia, letting out a loud sigh. "It always goes by too fast."

"I thought you liked school," said Ruby.

"I do. But I like vacation just as much."

"This summer seemed really long to me," said Flora.

"Me, too," said Nikki. "But I still don't want to go back to school."

"Why not?" asked Ruby. "School's fun. You get to be with your friends."

"*You* don't *have* friends yet," Flora said to Ruby. "I mean, friends your own age."

"I do, too. Lacey is my age. Almost. And I'll have more friends soon. Nikki, how come you don't want to go to school?"

Nikki shrugged. "I just don't."

"Not even if you and Flora and I will be in the same class?" asked Olivia, who knew why Nikki didn't want to go to school. It must have been awful to be a Sherman in Camden Falls. The Shermans had an unfortunate reputation, mainly because Mr. and Mrs. Sherman drank too much and Mr. Sherman had a terrible temper. The three Sherman kids showed up at school in ill-fitting clothes and were able to bathe only when the plumbing in their little house was in working order. Olivia hoped school might improve for Nikki now that they were all friends.

"Well, that will make it better," Nikki agreed. "Plus, we'll have Mrs. Mandel."

Every student at Camden Falls Elementary hoped to get Mrs. Mandel for sixth grade.

The girls lounged on the couches until Nikki looked at the Needle and Thread clock.

"Oh!" she cried. "I have to go! I promised Tobias I'd get home by three to take care of Mae so he can go to work. He got a part-time job at John's."

"John's?" said Flora.

"That auto body place out by the new grocery store." Nikki jumped to her feet. "Okay. I'll see you guys at school tomorrow. Wish me luck on the bus."

"Good luck," said Flora and Ruby dutifully.

And Olivia said, "Stick with Mae. Maybe no one will bother you if you're sitting with a first-grader."

The door closed behind Nikki, and Flora felt in her pocket for the photograph. Then she glanced at her sister. "Hey, Ruby. If you'll go to Ma Grand-mère to get chocolate chip cookies for you and Olivia and me, I'll pay for the cookies."

"Cool," said Ruby, who grabbed the money from her sister and was out the door before Flora could change her mind.

Flora scooted down the couch to Olivia and thrust the photo in front of her. "Look. Look at this," she said.

"What is it?" Olivia squinted at the picture of a young woman posing stiffly with a little girl.

"I found it in this box of papers that was in the attic," Flora replied. "I haven't told anyone about the box yet," she added, squirming slightly. "It's old family stuff and I kind of want to keep it a secret."

"Min's stuff? How come you want to keep it a secret?"

"I just do."

"Okay. . . . Who are these people?"

"That's just the thing. I've been looking at the picture over and over, thinking the woman is familiar. The little girl is my mother when she was four years old. See?" Flora turned over the photo to show Olivia the writing on the back. "It says 'Frannie and Mary — nineteen seventy.' Frannie is my mother. And at first I thought Mary might be Min's sister, Mary Elizabeth. A nice photo of my mother with her aunt. But take a look at the necklace Mary is wearing."

Olivia brought the photo closer to her face and gazed at it for a moment. Then she screamed and dropped the picture to the floor.

"*Shh!*" hissed Flora. She grabbed for the photo and turned around to look at Min and Gigi, but they were busy talking with the UPS woman who had arrived at the back door with a delivery. Then she clasped Olivia's hand. "It's who I think it is, isn't it?" she said quietly.

"Scary Mary," whispered Olivia, "wearing her star necklace."

"What was my mother doing with Mary Woolsey? I didn't think Mary knew my family back then."

"I have no idea," Olivia croaked, and she cleared her throat.

"Really? You don't have any idea at all? You've told me everything you know about Mary?"

"Cross my heart. She's, like, eighty years old. She lives alone — you saw her house. She's possibly a witch and definitely crazy. She's buried some kind of treasure in her garden and she keeps a child hidden in her basement."

Flora narrowed her eyes at Olivia.

"Okay, those are just rumors. But they might be true."

"What else?"

"She catches rats in her attic and fries them up for dinner?" suggested Olivia.

"Come on. Tell me something that will help."

"I don't know anything more. I mean, anything more than you do. She comes here three times a week to take in people's mending and stuff, and to return it to them when it's finished. She's been doing that ever since the store opened, I think, and that's how she earns her money, thanks to Gigi and Min." Olivia looked at the photo again and shuddered. "I really don't know what she would have been doing with your mother." She paused. "Maybe your mother had a secret past."

Flora was about to reply when Ruby entered the store, holding aloft a paper bag from Ma Grand-mère. Flora stuffed the picture back in her pocket and whispered to Olivia, "We can discuss this later."

Now she had even more questions . . . and no answers. Although she did like the idea of someone, anyone, having a secret past.

New adventures are right around the corner!

Main Street

#2: Needle and Thread

Thanksgiving comes to Camden Falls—and Flora is worried about spending it without her parents. Ruby hopes to get a part in the school musical. And Olivia and Nikki have problems of their own.

But the bond that ties the friends together will also give them strength to work things out—one stitch at a time.

Coming in August!

■SCHOLASTIC

www.scholastic.com